CAULDRONS AND CONFESSIONS

Warlocks MacGregor®

MICHELLE M. PILLOW

Michelle M. Pillow® - MichellePillow.com

About Cauldrons and Confessions

PARANORMAL MAGICK SCOTTISH
CONTEMPORARY ROMANCE

Malina MacGregor is more than just a delicate flower in need of manly protection, but you wouldn't know if by the slew of male family members who show up anytime she tries to go on a date. Sure, she's made some poor choices in men in the past—like the demon she mistakenly hooked up with in Las Vegas years ago. But that was then, and this is now, and she more than made up for that mistake.

Darragh "Dar" Lahey may be a luck demon, but his luck ran out the night he met the temptress —Malina. Now he's back, and he has an axe to grind. Malina needs to pay for what she did to him, and the supernatural attacks he's firing at her magickal family is just the beginning. There is only one hitch in his plans for revenge—even after all this time the stubborn woman can still make his heart ache, and his body burn with need.

Warning: Contains yummy, hot, mischievous MacGregors who are almost certainly up to no good on their quest to find true love.

Warlocks MacGregor Series

SCOTTISH MAGICKAL WARLOCKS

Love Potions

Spellbound

Stirring Up Trouble

Cauldrons and Confessions

Spirits and Spells

Kisses and Curses

Magick and Mischief

A Dash of Destiny

Night Magick

More Coming Soon

Visit www.MichellePillow.com for details.

To all those who need a little magical mischief in their lives. Be careful what you wish for. Uncle Raibeart is (still) looking for love.

Note from the Author

The term "warlock" is a variation on the Old English word "waerloga" primarily used by the Scots. It meant traitor, monster, deceiver, or other variations. The MacGregor Clan does not look at themselves as being what history has labeled their kind. To them, warlock means magick, family, and immortality. This book is not meant to be a portrayal of modern day witches or those who have such beliefs. The MacGregors are a magickal class all their own.

As with all my books, this is pure fantasy. In real life, please always practice safe sex and magic(k).

Chapter One

NEVADA DESERT, 1960

"How did you find me?" Malina couldn't meet her brother's gaze, but she felt Niall staring at her in disappointment from across the car as he drove her further and further away from Las Vegas. Eventually, the bright lights of the city faded in the rearview mirrors to an insignificant spot on the horizon. On any other night, the view might have been beautiful.

"Do ya really think you're hard to track?" Niall gave a sarcastic laugh that held no humor. His Scottish accent was a stark contrast to her softer English one.

Malina tapped her fingers against the soda bottle on her lap not drinking it. Her eyes focused on the hem of his kilt. For once his clothes had blended in. When he came for her at the hotel, people assumed he was a performer, not the evil-hunting warlock he actually was. If there was an evil threat to be dealt with, there was no better man than Niall.

"The family always knows where ya are," he continued. "Da sent me to bring ya home. Mobsters and degenerates are not the company for a lady to keep. I must say I'm disappointed in ya, Malina. A warlock of your abilities and ya squander it on booze and losers. Sometimes I think ma made a mistake sending ya away from the clan during the witch trials. Ya were a baby, so in some ways, it was not your fault that ya don't fully understand the concept of family loyalty and duty. However, at over three hundred years old ya should know better."

His words stung, but she had no defense. It's not like she needed to be reminded that she was an outsider because of some humans in East Lothian, Scotland decided witches needed to be burned at the stake when she was born. One look at the birthmark on her ass and they would have declared her the child of Satan. Their beloved Aunt Elspeth had sacrificed herself so that Malina could live. The family liked to remind her of that fact as well.

"When are you going to give up these silly rebellions? I think ya get some sick pleasure in making us rescue ya. Is that it?" he demanded. "How many more will there be, Malina? How many bad decisions and stupid mistakes? Lord Barrison, the rogue—"

"That was the seventeen hundreds," she protested.

"My point exactly. Barrison was trying to get ya to Gretna Green to elope for our family money. The cardsharp in London whose name we could never fully ascertain. George, the horse thief. Billy, the cattle rustler. Jack, the moonshiner. Your life has been a repeat of the same bad judgments. And now ya have graduated to mass murderers." Niall jerked the car roughly to the right to avoid a cactus.

Malina slid on the seat and had to grab the door to right herself. The dots of blood on her hand reminded her of the casino shooting she'd just witnessed. The blood stained her fancy dress. Malina began picking at her hand to scrape it off. The agony was almost too much. "I didn't know he..." She couldn't say the words.

When Niall first came to her to tell her the man she was with was a demon, she hadn't wanted to believe him. She'd demanded proof. It was because of her all those people had been hurt and probably killed. If she had let Niall stop the demon sooner, those innocent people would have been safe.

"That's my point. Ya never know, and ya never think. Each and every time ya have called me to help ya, and each time ya didn't know he was a bad guy. Tell me, how could ya not know that the man ya were with is a demon?" Niall took a deep breath. "Drink it."

"His name is Dar," she said, not liking the word demon.

"Drink it," he repeated.

"I don't want to," Malina denied. Just hours before she had been so happy. Now the pain was unbearable. This was much worse than the time she'd ben duped by a gold digging rogue. Barrison had wanted her money. Dar wanted her family's magick. Oh, and he had done such a great job making her fall for him so that the betrayal of who he was combined with the ache of loss in her chest. It had all been a lie—every single second.

The headlights revealed the long stretch of

endless desert, a wasteland of cacti and sand. After they had passed a rundown service station, the road disappeared, and the ride became bumpy.

A tear slipped down her cheek. "What are you going to do, Niall?"

"Ya know what I have to do," Niall answered. "Now drink it. We're almost there. I don't want the demon taking possession of ya. I would not be able to live with myself if I was forced to subdue ya."

"Maybe we're wrong," she said, though the logic of what she'd seen contradicted her vain hope. "Maybe he can explain himself."

"He's a demon," Niall stated as if that was all the proof he needed. "What other proof do ya need? If my word is not good enough, then ya saw what he did."

He stopped the car a little too quickly, and she was thrust toward the dash. She gripped the soda bottle as liquid splashed over the top.

He was right. She'd messed up this time, worse than ever before. She was a poor excuse for a warlock. All this time she acted like she had something to prove, that she was just as good as all her brothers, and cousins, and the entire

MacGregor clan, and really she was the outcast screw up. She didn't even know a demon when it pinched her on the witch's mark.

"Trust your family," Niall insisted. "Family is the only thing ya can count on in this life, my sister."

Malina chugged the warm liquid laced with magical herbs. The numbness took effect almost instantly, and she felt herself calming and becoming more compliant. Mumbling as if she was suddenly under the influence of an entire bottle of tequila, she said, "Niall, this doesn't feel like a protection spell. I feel... strange."

"It's for your own good. That will make this easier. I promise I'll keep my word. None of the others will ever know what ya did. Trust me. We'll clean up this mess and then it will be like it never happened. I'll take care of ya. I will always take care of ya," Niall said, taking the empty bottle from her. "Now, get out of the car. We have a demon to kill."

Malina blinked a few times before obeying. Everything became a white fog as she met Niall by the trunk of the car. Her limbs hung heavy at her sides. Her eyes became fixated on the trunk as it opened. Dark eyes met hers. Those eyes didn't reflect evil. They appeared frightened, and a little angry. Dar didn't look like a demon. He looked like a man—a man tied up in the back of a car in the middle of the desert at night. Maybe they were wrong. Maybe this didn't have to be done.

A gag pulled tight to Dar's handsome mouth, muffling his words as he tried to speak. Malina couldn't be sure if it were a plea or a curse.

"It's as we discussed back at the hotel. He'll try to trick you. The evil ones always do. You must not believe their lies." Niall drew a sharp knife from his waist. The carved steel gleamed as Niall's magick swirled up from his hand. He reached for Dar, using magick to strengthen his grip as he pulled the man from the trunk and began dragging him around to the front of the vehicle.

Niall pointed the blade at the ground and began to chant under his breath. Sand swirled over the desert as it lifted up and flew into the sky to create a grave.

"Wait." Malina tried to bring up her powers, but they were slow to come to her. "Are you sure? He looks human."

Niall didn't wait, didn't listen as if he knew she'd lose her nerve. He thrust the demon blade into Dar. The man's once handsome face morphed into a hideous beast, giving her the last shred of evidence she needed. Kind eyes darkened into black pits as horns grew from his head. She screamed, backing up so quickly she tripped over the car. Niall didn't miss a beat. He threw the demon into the hole and lifted his hand to create fire. Within seconds, Dar was burning, and the smell of his death was wafting over her numbed senses.

Confusion and pain filled her, combining with embarrassment. Niall was right. She'd fucked up yet again. She pushed to her feet and stumbled to the graveside. The smell was overwhelming, and she gagged. "I don't feel well." The red fire in the pit roared angrily as she looked down into it. She wanted to jump in and die too. "I feel dizzy."

Tonight, life as she knew it had ended. There was no coming back from the feeling of loss she felt. Blackness came for her, and she didn't fight it. She didn't care if she never woke up again.

Chapter Two

GREEN VALLIS, WISCONSIN, PRESENT DAY

Malina MacGregor opened her eyes as a sensation of panic surged through her chest. She tried to catch her breath, gasping, "ten-Mississippi, nine-Mississippi..." as she focused on anything that would calm her racing heart. It had been decades since anxiety of this magnitude had held her in its grip. She couldn't recall what she'd been dreaming of, or if she'd been dreaming at all.

One thing was for certain. Something powerful had affected her magick deeply.

Her left hand tingled, and then it began to shake. Her breathing was ragged, and she had a hard time catching it. She pushed out of the bed, kicking frantically at the covers. In fear, she lifted her fingers toward the window. Malina magickally forced it open without touching it. A cold rush of air filled her room, whipping her nightgown around her legs as she moved nearer the window. She took several deep breaths and forced herself to calm down.

It was still night. The expansive lawn of the MacGregor mansion appeared untouched. A hill sloped gently down toward the valley below. Melting snow dripped from moonlit branches on centuries-old oak trees that ran along the driveway. Her brothers' cars lined one side of the cobblestone. It was the only road in or out of the estate. Behind the house were six acres of gardens with winding paths. Someone would have to trek through a lot of forest to find their way back there.

The Georgian mansion towered above the town like a feudal lord over his subjects. The people of Green Vallis might not know it, but the family of warlocks living over them had become their protectors. And, whereas they did not rule like a medieval lord over surfs, they did take responsibility for the townspeople's lives. For, where the MacGregors went, trouble followed. These innocent humans were not responsible, and thus should not be made aware that the problem even existed. For all they knew, an eccentric Scottish extended family had moved into town.

The MacGregors had only been in Green Vallis for a few years and already her brother, Erik, had fought a psychic shadow creature. The *lidérc* were nasty things that feasted on the emotional energy of their victims. Her brother, Iain, battled a banshee. They all had run-ins with ghosts, including her Uncle Fergus who had summoned the reincarnated spirit of his long-dead wife who wasn't too happy with the sloppy spells he'd been casting for the last century in his efforts to bring her back to life.

Even though such paranormal occurrences were common for her family, one thing about Wisconsin was not. Moving to Green Vallis had brought Erik, Iain, and Fergus their *fíorghrá*, true love. In battling these great threats, they'd somehow managed to find other pieces of their hearts—*pieces* that fitted naturally into the MacGregor family as if fate destined it.

Green Vallis was unlike other places they'd lived. Energy flowed from the ground in a convergence of ley lines. They all felt it and were stronger because of it. The danger of staying was that other supernatural creatures would feel the draw as well. Perhaps the panicked reaction she had was a warning that more trouble was on its way.

"What now?" she whispered, searching the grounds, even as the cold breeze stung her nose and lips.

The family owned nearly eighty acres in total, including the forest and a small stream in the woods. Malina glanced over the coach house built in the late eighteen hundreds. Her brothers wanted to convert it into a garage. But the heritage landmark was in full view of anyone curious enough to happen up the drive. Like the nosy Mrs. Callister who liked to tell the entire world in great detail anytime a MacGregor so much as moved a brick an inch. It was a conversion they'd do slowly so as not to arouse suspicion. It wouldn't do to have the historical building change overnight.

"Mrs. Callister is that you?" Malina mumbled, not really believing it was. The outbuilding showed no signs of life.

The house itself was over twenty thousand square feet with the total rooms numbering in the sixties. Magick protected the MacGregor estate thanks to her brother Euann's security spells. Even if those were to fail, her extended family was spread out over the house, so she wasn't worried about anything suspicious breaching the walls.

Yet, the feeling of anxiety wouldn't leave her.

The only other property on the hill was the Victorian house that belonged to her sister-in-law. Lydia was a green witch and ran a small business called *Love Potions* making homemade lotions, soaps, and candles. Malina wouldn't be able to see that far from her window. Was Lydia out in the forest harvesting herbs for her store again? Was this the week the woman was going to the lotion makers' convention with Erik?

As she peered through the shadows, her eyes failed to uncover the cause of the disturbance. Her intuition, however, whispered to the contrary. She closed her eyes and took a deep breath. It wasn't Lydia. Something felt off—not necessarily good or bad, just wrong. It was like the universe had shifted for a moment and then righted itself leaving one or more things askew. It was a nagging thought she couldn't express with words.

"Reveal yourself," she commanded softly.

Tiny blue lights rose from the Earth. The

small pinpoints around the tree would have been birds. A larger light in the forest could have been a deer. From below in the valley, a great many lights floated up, the life force of the people living in town at the bottom of the hill. Only one light gave her pause. Someone was trapped in the trunk of Euann's car.

"What did you do now?" she grumbled at her brother, even though he wasn't present to hear it. With a frown, she grabbed a robe from the end of her king-size bed and slipped it over her arms as she went downstairs to investigate.

MacGregor Mansion, so all the local towns-folk nicknamed the property, was perhaps one of her favorite homes they'd had over the years. Some members of the clan had wanted to move the family back to Scotland, to their ancestral homeland. In reality, they were legally Americans and, in the age of the Internet, moving an entire clan might draw some worldwide attention they didn't want.

The New York penthouse had been nice, and she liked the constant stream of people, but there had been little nature to draw power from, and a warlock needed power to wield magick. In the South, the weather had been too hot, and she'd used half her magickal energy to stay dry in the humidity. The England of her youth had been lovely—or at least it was now that it resided in her memory—but she no longer recognized the country when she visited and found herself staring at the hints of the past she could find in old buildings and landscapes. Then there was Las Vegas in the 1960s. There was no way in hell she would ever set foot in that city again. Her memories of Vegas were a blur, and she had no desire to clear them, but she remembered enough never to go back.

Her hand began to tingle again, and she shook it vigorously to get it to stop. Perhaps she'd pinched a nerve and needed to have Cait tend to it when her aunt woke up in the morning. Cait had a knack for curing ailments.

Malina crept down the open marble staircase toward the front door. She made a small noise—surprised when she stepped on a clump of dirt at the bottom of the stairs. Someone must have tracked it in. It was then she realized she'd forgotten her slippers. Hopping a couple of times, she brushed her heel against her ankle to dust it off.

Malina felt her body attempting to draw

energy from the plant life outside. The family used nature to fuel their magick. Power needed to come from somewhere. It's not like magick could just appear out of thin air for no reason. Yet another reason Wisconsin was so perfect. It had plenty of countryside. Of course, sexual climax always gave a great power rush, but try bringing a man home for the night with a slew of brothers, male cousins, uncles, and her da waiting for them with arms crossed and magick at the ready for an Old Western showdown.

Even worse than the macho greeting party would be her ma, Margareta MacGregor, waiting with her horrible wedding planning scrapbook, and a disappointed lecture about being a lady. "Do not let men ride in the cart before they got the horse attached, Malina," or whatever it was her ma tried to impart with her stupid sayings. Like at over 425 years old Malina was going to be clinging to her precious maidenhead.

"That cherry rotted long ago," she muttered. She shivered as she stepped in snow. No wonder her body was trying to generate power, it was automatically keeping her warm. The white powder melted around her with each step making deep footprints.

Coming to the trunk of Euann's latest gadget-filled sports car, she pointed her finger to pop it open. It didn't budge as it repelled her magick back at her. She dodged the tiny blast, letting it disperse behind her. Why was a protection spell locking a body inside?

Sighing more in annoyance than anything else, she pounded her fist on the top. "Hey, everything all right in there?"

She leaned closer to listen. She wasn't sure why, but the idea of someone being locked in a trunk made her uneasy. Movement brushed the interior and then stopped. Malina thumped her fist again on the trunk. A return knock sounded from inside. She could think of no reason to trap an evil creature in the trunk of a new car. Some family idiot had probably locked himself inside.

Malina glanced around the lawn to make sure it was still empty. It was undoubtedly a useless precaution, but she did it anyway out of habit. Then, stepping back, she lifted both hands and concentrated on pulling Euann's car apart at the seams. Her magick found tiny holes in the protection spell. Whoever had cast the spell had been hasty, or lazy, in their implementation. Bolts floated in the air first with large chunks of metal following behind them. Finally, the trunk came apart. It was enough for the person trapped inside to free himself.

As the trunk lid moved out of the way, she was greeted with the way-too-intimate sight of Euann's naked ass as he bent away from her. She gasped and instinctively jerked back. The parts of Euann's car that were suspended in the air fell to the ground. Malina wasn't too worried about the crashing sound waking neighbors. Their only neighbor was Lydia, and she was used to the MacGregor chaos.

Euann grunted as he rolled over parts of his disassembled car scattered in the snow. He landed near her feet. His dark eyes appeared confused and unable to focus.

Malina lifted her hands as she tried not to see anything else that would scar her for the next century. Though, honestly, these days the MacGregor men seemed to be running around naked about as much as they wore clothes. They'd taken to streaking in the woods.

"What are you doing out here?" Malina demanded, tugging her robe closer to her body.

Euann hiccupped and started to laugh. She

detected the overpowering smell of tequila wafting from him. Figured. He was drunk.

"Rory told me it was my bed," Euann explained, "but I don't think he was telling the truth."

And that figured too. Her cousin had something to do with this nonsense.

Euann tried to push to his wobbly feet. The longer length of his dark hair plastered to the side of his face, wet from snow.

"And you're naked because...?" she prompted.

"Don't ya sleep naked?" Euann questioned as if she were the strange one. He looked at the ground for a very long moment, taking his time processing what was happening. "Hey, what did ya do to my car?"

"You're welcome, dumbass," Malina said by way of an answer. "Now get inside before you scare the wildlife. And for goodness sakes, please draw in a little power to produce heat before you turn blue."

Euann didn't listen to her advice as he began reaching for a piece of his car in the snow. "Put it back together."

Malina shrugged out of her robe and placed it on his shoulders before tugging his arm to walk with her. "Come on, brother, we'll see to it in the morning."

"Ya destroyed my car," he insisted. "I'm putting that in the revenge book. Don't think I won't. I love that car. She's my lady."

"You bespelled my dance partner at the 1876 ball and made him believe I had leprosy when he tried to kiss me. He left screaming. We'll call this even."

"Fair enough," Euann grumbled, as he struggled to thread his arms into her robe. He moved in a small circle as if chasing the sleeve hole. "But I like this car more than ya liked your date, more than ya like most of your dates."

"Fair enough," she agreed. He was right. "Care to tell me what has you drinking so much lately?"

"Aw, not ya, too, English rose. I get enough lectures from ma," Euann grumbled, his Scottish accent slurring.

Malina knew the nickname was meant as an endearment, but she had never liked it. Calling her English only reminded her that she had been banished from Scotland during the witch trials as a baby and raised away from the clan. It wasn't her fault that her accent was English, her mannerisms were English, and her way of thinking was English. Their pointing that out only served to set her apart from the rest of the family. At first, she'd tried to force the Scottish accent, but that only made their teasing worse.

"She's not awake, is she? I'm too drunk to lie effectively," Euann said. "You'll have to cover for me."

"You're sleeping naked in your car in the middle of winter," Malina pointed out. She pushed her magick over him to keep him warm. "Maybe someone needs to lecture you a little about your life choices."

"Don't ya ever get tired?" Euann asked, his eyes turning toward the ground as he took a concentrated step. "Or lonely?"

"We live with a houseful of relatives. When do you have a chance to be lonely?" Malina guided him to the front door.

He stopped and slid his arm around her shoulders. The robe fell open, and she grimaced as she drew the front flaps together and held them in her fist to keep him from flashing.

"Don't pretend ya don't know what I'm talking about. I see the hollow in your eyes." He touched the bridge of her nose. "Perhaps it's something to do with turning 500 soon. We'll officially be old. Unmarried. We'll turn into crazy Uncle Raibeart, proposing to every woman we meet, drunk, lost, naked, pathetic."

Malina gave a small laugh. "You're halfway there. If you want, I can slip you a love potion and send you after Mrs. Callister. Then you won't be so lonely. And maybe then she'll stop following all of us around town taking notes and posting pictures on her blog. She seems to like you the best out of all of us."

"Oh, och, not funny." Euann winced. Then, laughing, he suggested, "How about we hit Niall with it? We can watch him trail after the town busybody. I'd give up casting spells for a year to watch him make a lovesick ass out of himself, singing and whatnot on that old biddy's lawn."

"It'd probably kill half the town to hear Niall belt out love songs," Malina added. "It is about time our brother lightened up a little. All that time alone hunting supernatural bad-asses has made him surly."

"Do ya ever think we'll find it?" Euann asked.

"Find what?"

"What Jane and Iain have. What Erik and

Jane have," Euann mumbled. "What Uncle Fergus and Donna and Elspeth have."

"I think you mean what Lydia and Erik have. Otherwise, the family dynamic suddenly turned weirder than usual." Malina attempted to pull Euann up the staircase, but he slipped out of her grasp and sat on the bottom step. She magickally closed the front door and locked it.

"That's what I said, what Lydia and Jane have." Euann shut his eyes and laid his temple against an oak baluster. "My brothers are so lucky. We're never going to have that, Malina. Ya know that, don't ya? We're cursed."

The words stung, and she bit her lip. Euann didn't say it to be mean, so there was no reason to defend herself against his observation. In all honesty, he was probably right. She didn't believe she was worthy of finding true love. Some people were never meant to have such things. The loneliness threatened to consume her, and she pushed it aside. It was better not to dwell. There was a reason she didn't contemplate such things.

"Maybe if you talked to girls in person instead of meeting them on the Internet," Malina offered. "You're a handsome enough guy. I've seen your profile picture. Those women go crazy for you, call you their Latin boy-toy, man-candy, whatever it is they say."

"I'm Scottish," Euann needlessly argued. "Ma did not have an affair with a Sack Man. I can't help that I tan better than all of ya and look sexiest in a kilt."

"I'm not going to discuss which of my brothers is sexiest in a kilt," Malina stated.

"I know, right! Jane is experimenting with which plants help our powers the most. And Lydia is a green witch who belongs to... whoever. And they fit so well into the family, ya know," Euann mumbled drunkenly. "It makes sense that fate would send them. But we're the losers, Malina. Fate probably won't smile on this family like that for another 500 years. All the love has been given out. We'll be forced to settle or be hermits."

"There is nothing worse than a drunk making self-realizations and thinking everyone else cares to hear them," Malina muttered.

"What?" Euann leaned toward her as if that would help him comprehend her words better.

"And Donna cooking?" Malina asked instead, prodding along her brother's nonsense. "Did that use up our love luck, too?"

"Och, no, banshee. None of Donna's cooking. She tried to kill us last winter." Euann's eyes opened almost fearfully. "Uncle Fergus didn't cut their trip short, did he? Don't eat the cookies. They near killed Traitor. The poor dog didn't do anything to anybody."

"Ok," Malina agreed.

"No, I'm serious, Malina. Don't eat the cookies," Euann enunciated.

"I can see that," Malina patted his head. "I promise I won't go back in time and eat Donna's killer cookies. You have my word."

"Ah, dammit, Malina. Why did ya let him out?" Rory appeared at the top of the stairs in his pajama pants. Like most of the MacGregors, he had light brown hair and green eyes. He'd tipped his hair with blond streaks but kept it trimmed short. Right now, his hair stuck up around his head like a wild creature had attacked him in the night. He hurried barefoot down to the first floor while keeping an eye on the upstairs landing to make sure no one heard his descent. "I had good reason to lock him up."

"I love her," Euann slurred, whipping around toward the sound of their cousin's voice. He lost his balance and again grabbed hold of a baluster for support.

"No ya don't, ya daft twit," Rory grumbled. "And keep your voice down."

"I *could* love her," Euann persisted.

"Nice robe," Rory teased, before suddenly talking to Euann as he would a pet. "Whose a pretty boy? You're a pretty boy."

"What's going on here?" Malina eyed her cousin before turning back to Euann who was mumbling nonsensical sounds as if on the verge of passing out.

"The fool has got it into his head that he's in love with Charlotte. He says he's going to rescue her, aren't ya?" Rory nudged Euann with his toe. "Going to marry her and make her part of the clan, aren't ya, lover boy? Euann's going to save Charlotte and make her sane again with his love."

Euann swatted at Rory's foot, missing his target and hitting the steps instead. He yelped in pain. "I can save her. Then Niall won't try to erase any more of her memories. She won't turn out like Helena. It's the right thing. We have to do the right thing, or we'll never lift the curse."

Malina shared a look with Rory. Charlotte was Lydia's best friend. When their magick had gone awry, they ended up erasing the woman's memories for the sake of her sanity. If they hadn't, Charlotte would have been on a one-way trip to an asylum. Unfortunately, there had been a great deal of magickal exposure, and Charlotte wasn't the same afterward. They were doing everything they could to help navigate the poor woman back to mental stability.

"Did Niall say he was taking more from her?" Malina asked. "We can't do that."

Rory gestured that he didn't have the answers.

"He has to be, right? He's been following her and even moved into the apartment next to her so he could watch her. Why else would he stay in this town for so long?" Euann reasoned. "Niall does not care who he sacrifices if it is in the name of protecting the clan from whatever he perceives to be a—hey, your hair is brown!"

Euann reached for Malina's locks as if he was seeing them for the first time. She swatted his hand back. "No thanks to you, brother."

He laughed. "I gave ya gray hair that kept coming back. Ya have to admit that was a good spell."

Rory started to snicker. "Aye, and she looked like a banshee."

Malina arched a brow and shot her cousin an irritated look. "Don't encourage him."

"I'll stop if ya let me have Jim," Rory offered.

Malina sighed. "Jim" was what her cousin had named his non-existent pet boxer puppy that he wanted Malina and Jane to magickally materialize for him. Jane's unique heritage made her like a nature-battery power source, and Malina's ability to materialize objects into reality from pictures had given Rory the grand idea that they should make him a friend. She had nothing against dogs. In fact, she quite liked them. The entire family did. Fergus's English bulldog, Traitor, had been living with the MacGregors for decades. The problem was Rory's dream dog came from a giant billboard he'd stolen and would be ten times the normal size of a natural dog.

Very flatly, she answered, "No."

"Shh, Rory, we can't call her banshee anymore. Jane's ma was a banshee." Euann leaned his head against the banister and closed his eyes. "And now she is a tree."

"Should we carry him to bed?" Malina sighed heavily, not wanting to haul her brother up the stairs. "Do you think we can do it without waking everyone in the house?"

"I'm not going to bed," Euann said. "I'm going to find Charlotte."

"No reason." Rory lifted his hand. Yellow light moved over Euann as Rory petrified his cousin into place. "There. He'll stick to that spindle until morning. I'm too tired to keep running after him."

"We're not supposed to petrify each other anymore. You heard what the elders said." Malina glanced along the upper landing to make sure no one had detected what had happened.

"I won't tell if ya won't," Rory offered.

"I think they might notice when they get up in the morning." Malina gestured to the front hall where Euann was noticeable from several vantage points.

"They have yet to bind any of our powers, and they've been threatening for centuries," Rory dismissed. "Ugh, could ya imagine it if they did?"

"Imagine being human?" Malina shook her head. "I used to wish it when I was young and naïve. Now it sounds like a nightmare. Not being able to move traffic when you're running late? Or what about cleaning everything by hand even if you don't want to? Having to go to an actual store to buy my clothes?" She shivered. "No thank you."

"I'm always more worried about not being able to defend myself from a supernatural attack, or not sensing when other supernatural creatures are nearby. Or what if we got sick, like people sick, and had to be put in the hospital at the whims of doctors?" Rory led the way up the stairs, his steps slow. "It's a wonder humans survive at all."

A small shiver worked its way over Malina, and she glanced at the front door. Her hand tingled, and she balled it into a fist. "Do you feel that?"

"What? Is it Aunt Margareta?" Rory frowned in worry as he looked around the room. Then, laughing when he didn't see anyone, he said, "Good one. Ya got me. Made me look."

Malina managed a small smile as if that had been her intent though it hadn't. The strange feeling seemed to radiate from outside the door. It wasn't her brother locked in the trunk that had woken her from her sleep.

"Did you have to leave him naked?" Malina grumbled as they reached the top of the staircase. "That was my favorite robe, and now I'll have to burn it."

Rory chuckled. "He insisted. Ya know us warlocks, any reason to take off our clothes."

"Some things are best left unseen." Malina lifted her hand to wave good night and turned from him to make her way back to bed.

That night she didn't sleep as the window drew her back to its cold panes to stare at the moonlit yard. She did not leave it open, liking that the glass separated her from whatever lingered beyond. Shadows moved, stretching and contracting to mark the passing of time.

Euann's word echoed through her thoughts. *"We're never going to have that, Malina. Ya know that, don't ya? We're cursed."*

"Cursed," she whispered against the glass. Her breath fogged the window, and she traced her fingertip in the shape of a heart through it. When she drew back, she watched as the form took on a life of its own. A streak of moisture ran down the glass, breaking the heart in half. Both sides of the image slid downward before falling onto the floor and dissipating.

She was unsure if it was her magick or some outside force who'd created the illusion.

"Reveal yourself," she commanded.

The blue lights rose from the Earth as they

had before, only this time magick showed a life force standing near the old oak tree on the front lawn. It was too dark to see if it was animal or human, but her hand trembled as it had before. Fear welled inside her, and she forced herself away from the window. Like a coward, she crawled into bed, pulled the covers over her head, and tried not to move. The dark cocoon did not make her feel better.

Chapter Three

The attractive woman in the window called to the darkness within the demon, stirring all the hate and vengeance and anger he'd carried for decades. Finally, he'd found her. This time he was strong enough to fight. This time he wouldn't be fooled by a pretty face and sweet smile.

Her. The warlock. Malina MacGregor. Fucking bitch.

If he closed his eyes, he could still feel the sensation of being consumed by fire as he clawed his way from the fire realm back to Earth. He held on to that anger and hurt. It had kept him going over the long years.

Oh, but she still had her looks. Time had been very kind to her. The messiness of sleep did not diminish the loveliness of her light brown hair. It was the exact shade he remembered running through his fingers.

No. Dammit it all to hell. He was angry. Not horny. He would not let the temptress win this time.

Dar told himself he wanted to strike, to tear her flesh apart as she walked through snow, to make the white turn red. He wanted to shake her, and scream at her, and make her beg for his forgiveness. She didn't even bother to hide her powers as she pulled apart a car. Not like when he'd first met her. Then she'd been a cautious little liar, hiding the old magick in her veins and pretending to be something she wasn't. She'd even faked a British accent.

She'd tricked him, stole his luck, and condemned him to burn.

To strike now would be stupid. All the luck in the universe wouldn't help him if he went into a house full of warlocks half-cocked. His powers took time, and luckily he had a natural patience for the long game.

Ok, to be honest, he *normally* had patience. Malina stirred something inside him that made him act crazy and rash. Even after all these years, he wanted nothing more than to go to her and grab her and ask her why and beg and...

Fuck!

No. He must resist her temptations. He would not fall for her spells again. He reminded himself that what he really wanted was to watch her luck sour as a big gust of wind blew her off the side of a building.

Patience is a virtue.

That was what people said. He needed to wait and let his powers do the rest.

Already he could sense her luck turning. Dar wasn't the only supernatural power stirring in the woods tonight. Other forces were coming to play, and they wanted the MacGregors to suffer worse than he had. They needed to learn they couldn't get away with what they did. Consequences had actions.

Dar turned his attention to the tree line. Ghosts gathered amongst the branches. The ethereal forms focused on the house as if they'd discovered the cure for death.

A small goblin poked his head out of the ground only to disappear as he burrowed into the earth. The snow melted, and the soil darkened above the foul creature. Tiny fairies were attracted to the mound like flies to manure. The gnarled beings swarmed, an angry horde of stinging pests ready to do some damage.

"We want to play, we want to sin, but those MacGregors won't let us in."

Dar glanced down at the two childlike ghosts by his side who had spoken in unison. He saw beyond their sweet ringlet disguises to the small hellions lurking underneath. Lifting his left hand, he lightly patted their heads and watched as his power infused them. "Don't worry, dolls. I have a feeling your luck is about to change."

The other apparitions turned their attention toward him. The two spirits giggled and began skipping toward the mansion's front door. Some of the spectral images flashed violently in their eagerness to play. Others merely floated like benign silk tethered in the breeze.

The sound of the children's haunting voices drifted over the quiet lawn. "You can't hide. You can't seek. You can't find the will to speak. We're not bound anymore. We're not leaving like before."

The ghosts followed the children, squeezing through the tiniest of holes in the protective barriers the MacGregors had cast. One by one they slowly passed over the lawn toward the mansion as they made their journey to the front door.

Dar smiled at the chaos he'd unleashed and gingerly progressed toward the goblin mound. "Come out and play little friend." He waited for the goblin to show his face. The fairies scattered up into the night sky only to drift back down as they determined he meant no harm. "Step right up, ladies and ghouls. This round of luck is on me. Get it while it's hot."

Chapter Four

Malina kept her eyes averted as she tried to find something nice to say about the tofu, coriander, and goat cheese omelet that Aunt Cait placed before her. The woman looked as if she'd stepped out of 1950's television, where homemakers wore dresses and always looked perfect in their cashmere and pearls, whether baking a cake, cleaning the house, or receiving guests in the parlor. Though much older than Malina, Cait could have passed as her sister.

Malina bounced the back of her fork off the eggs a couple of times. "I should get ma. I'm sure she'd want to try this." As she made a move to stand, and hopefully escape, Cait dashed her hopes of fleeing the scene.

"Your da took her on a much-needed break to Budapest. They found a healer that can help with her regeneration." Cait motioned to the food. "This one is all yours."

"The table setting is lovely," Malina tried to distract Cait's attention by noting the magazine-like quality of her aunt's decor. Red and gold leaves coated with fake white snow created a centerpiece. The place settings were delicate bone china with red leaves along the edges.

"*Go raibh míle maith agat*," Cait thanked her. "Now eat. I have more in the kitchen if ya want seconds."

Every few decades Cait decided to try her hand at experimental gourmet cooking—without the aid of her powers. Apparently, this decade was tofu. Last decade had been molecular gastronomy. Malina wasn't averse to the finer things in life, but each dish had showcased a bubbly pile of what could only be called spittle.

Malina had the misfortune to be the first to walk into the expansive dining room and now sat alone with Cait's full attention on her. She took a gold napkin and slid it onto her lap, wishing Rory would stumble in as a distraction. When that didn't happen, she had no recourse but to choke a bite down. "It's, ah, spongy."

Cait arched a brow, and the lights began to flicker.

"I mean... unique?" Malina halfheartedly corrected as she gave a meaningful glance to the antique light fixture. The lights flicked harder as if someone turned the switch on and off to create a strobe light effect. "Delicious. I mean delicious."

"You're a horrible liar," Cait scolded. She slid the plate in front of her and used Malina's fork to try a piece. She sighed heavily. "It does taste like a wet sponge."

"It had a very nice color," Malina offered.

"I don't understand why my food never turns out. I do everything the books say." Cait tossed the plate over her shoulder and the discarded breakfast, plate and all, disappeared before it hit the ground. "Ya can stop flickering the lights now. I'm not going to make ya eat it."

Malina frowned. "Me? I'm not doing that. I thought it was you."

Cait shook her head in denial.

Malina shared a worried look with her aunt. Simultaneously, they turned their attention toward the kitchen. Rushing through the dining room, they were greeted by a floating pot the second they turned the corner. The dirty cooking utensils Cait had used to make her creation stood up from the counter. One by one, they flew through the air—a whisk, a fork, a measuring spoon, and a paring knife. The objects flung violently, hitting the wall next to Malina's head.

"You enchanted the cookware?" Malina questioned in disbelief, dodging a can opener.

"They weren't doing that when I left," Cait insisted. She lifted her hand as if to scold a naughty child. The objects didn't stop. Malina tried to use her magick to help subdue a toaster oven. The action only appeared to make the appliance mad as its door snapped open and closed. Flour dust began flinging itself into the air. Malina sneezed and backed away.

The sound of footsteps running upstairs reverberated through the ceiling. They moved toward the front staircase only to trip as someone stumbled and fell.

"Ow!" Rory's cry came from the direction of the foyer.

"Heavens to Betsy, what is happening in this house?" Cait yelled as she led the charge into the front hall. The possessed kitchen appliances and utensils continued their wayward journeys but thankfully didn't follow them out of the room.

The light fixture in the dining room swung back and forth as if blown by a strong wind but was no longer flickering. Malina tripped on what should have been open walk space. Her body flung forward, barely missing Cait's back as she crashed into a chair and then fell on the ground. She grabbed her sore foot and turned to see what she'd run into. A car muffler had been left on the dining room floor.

"What the...?" Malina frowned. If she wasn't mistaken, the soft sound of laughter came from somewhere in the shadows underneath the tabletop.

"Get it off," Rory yelled in pain. The tone of his voice was distinctive. He wasn't playing around. "Ow. Stop!"

Malina scrambled to her feet and hurried to help her cousin. She found Cait trying to grab the ends of a flapping blanket as it wrapped itself around Rory's head and chest. The harder Rory struggled, the tighter the blanket wrapped around him, suffocating him.

"Why have all the inanimate objects in this house gone mad?" Cait asked.

Malina glanced at the stairs to see if maybe Euann was getting revenge for being locked in the trunk. Her brother was still petrified, but his eyes were moving side to side in desperation as if watching something. She came closer to see a fairy's backside poking out from inside his ear. She pinched the pesky creature and jerked it out, tossing it toward the front door. Euann closed his eyes briefly in thanks. Another fairy poked its head out from a mess of his dark brown hair.

"You're infested." Malina flinched, slapping her hand through his hair and down his back, plucking off wayward fairies and tossing them aside. "Why is this happening? Fairies and enchanted objects? This makes no sense."

"Ach, damn temptresses!" Uncle Raibeart stumbled in from outside. The front door crashed open in his exuberance. He was mostly naked except for a tattered kilt he held around his waist like a towel. Mud smeared his flesh. Though he normally looked a little crazy, he appeared even more so now. He animated his tale with wide, sweeping gestures, and almost dropped his kilt. "Lured me from my bed and had me arse out in the woods thinking it was a bordello. I almost infused Lydia's tree mom with a wee bit of the ole magick stick if ya ken what I'm sayin'. Thankfully the sun came out and broke the enchantment, or I'd be picking splinters out of some verra bad places. Also, who put the tires on the roof? One nearly blew off and belted me on the head. The ladies of the house aren't going to appreciate that decorating choice."

"Raibeart, help me," Cait demanded. "The blanket is trying to kill Rory."

"What's this?" Raibeart looked around at his family, slowly registering the surrounding chaos. "Aw, now, who let the ghosts in?"

"Ghosts?" Malina swatted her hands in the air as the discarded fairies tried to attack her instead.

"Aye, ghosts," Raibeart motioned toward the blanket holding Rory down. "Two there." He gestured up the stairs. "Some there." He pointed toward the dining room. "There."

"I can't see anything." Malina looked around but detected no spirits.

Raibeart began mumbling an old incantation in Gaelic before adding, "Into the attic where ghost guests stay."

Almost instantly the chaos stopped, except for the fairies. However, when the creatures saw the distractions had left and all the MacGregors focused attention on them, they made a beeline for the dining room to hide.

"What was that about?" Cait unwrapped Rory and helped him to his feet.

Malina searched her brother's hair for any residual pests. Rattles and thumps sounded above them. "Why did you send them to the attic?"

"Where else would ya have me put them? Your room?" Raibeart snorted.

"I'd have you put them out of the house," Malina said.

"Were ya not listening? I was practically drained dry by temptress spirits. I didn't have enough juice to evict that many ghosts," Raibeart answered.

"How did they get in? I woke up to the blanket being held down over my head and something hitting me with a candlestick." Rory lifted his arm to show the bruises forming on his ribs. Raibeart tried to poke his finger at the tender flesh, and Rory slapped him back.

The noises above them grew louder. Cait frowned. "We can't stay here. Not with everyone gone. If we're going to get rid of the ghosts, we'll need more firepower."

"What do ya mean everyone is gone?" Rory asked.

"Margareta and Angus left for Budapest yesterday. Murdoch is on a meditation retreat and can't be easily reached. Erik took Lydia to a trade show in Cincinnati. Iain and Jane are communing with nature."

"Communing?" Rory repeated, with a confused look.

Malina and Cait gave him a pointed expression, waiting for him to catch up.

"They're rocking the old *birlinn*," Raibeart explained. "And when it's a rockin', ya better get to sockin', or else ya will be dockin' the dinghy."

"What does that even mean?" Malina asked, before quickly holding up her hand. "No. Never mind. Don't explain."

"*Birlinn?* Wow. Ya are so old," Rory teased.

"At least I didn't get attacked by me blankie," Raibeart retorted.

"What about Niall?" Malina asked Cait. "Is he at his apartment? We can all crash with him while we figure this out."

"Leprechaun outbreak," her aunt replied. "Colonies are popping up in Kansas and Oklahoma. They're causing earthquakes."

"Again?" Rory frowned. "Didn't he just deal with leprechauns?"

"You're thinking chupacabras," Malina corrected. "And what do you expect? There was a lot of rain last year, and those things mate like rabbits on speedballs."

"What's a speedball?" Cait asked.

"A game Americans play," Rory lied.

"Not the kind of speedball I meant," Malina muttered.

Rory smirked. The sounds in the attic became more restless as the spirits attempted to come downstairs. All eyes turned upward.

"We need to find out how they came inside in the first place," Malina said. "Euann's security spells have never been breached, not like this, never by so many."

Euann made a small moaning noise, which could have been a thank you, or an affront that his spells could even have been considered as a contributing cause to the current situation.

A foul odor wafted from the dining room.

"Oh, not nice at all. What did ya bake this time, Cait?" Raibeart demanded, holding his nose. "Testicular stew?"

"Goblin," Rory stated.

"Ya cooked a goblin? Good gods woman, why?" Raibeart cried in shock.

"No, *goblin*," Rory pointed to the dining room door. The squat creature waddled into the foyer. The fumes of his stench were so bad Malina was certain she saw the stink coming from the foul being like heat off a blacktop.

"Oh, no, stop this nonsense at once!" Cait ordered no one in particular. "Goblin odor is impossible to get out. We'll have to burn the house down."

The nasty creature gave an evil laugh and began running around the room touching the walls to mark his new territory and spread his stench. In his foolhardiness, he tripped on a steering wheel and skidded over the marble on his stomach. His limbs flailed in the air as he bounced off a wall and headed the other direction.

"You can scream. You can cry. You can even wonder why." Two singsong children's voices came from above. At first, they were soft and light, an eerie melody that Malina strained to hear.

Malina searched the upper landing for a sign of where the sound originated.

"You can beg. You can pout. But your luck is running out," the girls continued, growing louder.

The light fixtures shook and trembled. The wood balusters on the staircase creaked and groaned as if threatening to splinter apart.

Cait lifted her hand, trying to keep the chandelier over the front hall from falling as it twitched violently above them. "They're too strong."

Malina pulled at the petrified Euann, urging his limbs to thaw from their stone-like state just enough to break him free from the creaking wood.

"This home is bigger than ours before. We all know what lies in store." Sudden streams of cold air swept down the stairs. The ambient temperature dropped close to twenty degrees in an instant. Malina caught glimpses of transparent faces and hands flowing past her. The ghosts were becoming more powerful, manifesting into denser forms. She flung her magick at one of the creatures to repel him back, but the man who had died sometime in the 1700s seemed to feed upon her energy, pulling her magick inside himself to grow stronger. He whooped loudly and began swinging his arms around in a sudden burst of liveliness.

Raibeart and Rory did the same, and their magick also appeared to fuel the undead nuisances. They shot several blasts, each one bringing the spirits more life. A woman in a prairie dress appeared, spinning in circles as she dove down the stairs headfirst. Two pretty girls with ringlets giggled, covering their mouths.

"They're feeding off us," Cait said. The ghost of a young boy began pinching at her backside. She gasped, flinging her hand behind her to try to block the youthful attack. Her fingers swept through the boy's, not making contact. "Stop using magick."

What could only be a homely prostitute in a cowboy hat took after Raibeart. Her hands disappeared to some very inappropriate places.

"Retreat, retreat," Raibeart yelled, sprinting for the front door. "She's minin' for gold and shrivelin' my nuggets!"

"Move," Rory ordered, thrusting Malina aside. He kicked the banister with the heel of his foot several times, loosening it enough to pull Euann's arm free. They maneuvered his stiff body, half carrying and half dragging it over the floor.

As they made it through the front door, the heavy wood slammed shut behind them. Eerie music began to play, and laughter resounded from within as the mansion's new tenants evidently threw themselves a housewarming party.

Breathing hard, Malina dropped her hold on

Euann. Her brother's body rocked on the snowy grass before settling in a strange position.

"What just happened?" Malina asked, watching as streaks of light zipped past the windows. One of them had gotten into her bedroom, and soon pieces of her designer clothing were flying out onto the lawn. She gasped, running to grab a few of her favorites as they fluttered down.

"I think we were just evicted," Rory answered.

Malina's arm tingled. The muscles twitched, and she dropped the clothes on the ground. The fear from the night before renewed itself and she slowly turned around in the yard. Something watched them. She felt it.

She walked toward the oak, lifting her hands to sense the landscape. The pain in her limb became worse, and she clutched her upper arm wondering what was wrong. With her heritage, she wasn't prone to human illnesses, but that didn't mean she couldn't suffer from some very nasty supernatural ones.

"I think he's coming out of it," Cait said, motioning at Euann. "Which one of ya did this?"

"I don't know how it happened," Rory lied. "Malina?"

Malina didn't answer.

"I think we have *gremians*, as well," Raibeart observed. "I've been seeing car parts littered all over the place and look." He pointed at Euann's disassembled car on the lawn. "They're starting to tear everything apart. They're worse than termites, and a helluva lot meaner."

Malina walked faster toward the tree. Her fear originated there, and she wasn't going to spend another second hiding under the covers like she had last night.

"Malina?" Rory called louder. "What are ya doing?"

She came to a stop and looked up into the branches before examining the trunk as her gaze moved downward. Nothing appeared out of the ordinary, except for the fact that leaves had sprouted when they should have been dormant for winter. She let her feelings guide her, forcing herself to look where she most didn't want to go. The prickling in her arm turned into a sharper pain, a strange premonition, but one she accepted. She followed the short path in the melting snow to a goblin hole. Mold grew over the mound. The yellow fungus cut a path straight to the house, most likely following the goblin as he'd burrowed underneath the ground to get inside.

"Who roused a goblin?" Rory wondered aloud. "Nothing about this makes sense. This feels more prankish than an actual attack. Do ya think Iain or Erik is having us on? Or your parents? Uncle Angus and Aunt Margareta left and then within hours all of this started. Or maybe the ghosts followed Elspeth's essence into Donna's body when Uncle Fergus summoned her back to him, and now they think that they can become corporeal again if they enter our house?"

Malina watched as the ghost of a 1920s farm-hand sauntered out of the forest. The spirit didn't appear to see them as it made his way along the drive to join the others. The farmhand's neck and arm bent at a strange angle as if he'd been mangled in death. He didn't bother to knock as he walked inside.

"Malina? What do ya think?" Rory insisted when she merely stared at the door where the latest ghost disappeared.

The feelings of dread inside her became more pronounced. Her heart beat so hard it felt like the organ wanted to tear out of her chest. Her stomach knotted until the sensation tightened and choked all the way up her throat. "I don't think this is a prank, Rory. I believe this is the beginning of something very bad. Very bad indeed."

Her breathing deepened, and she gripped her upper arm as the pain radiated from her hand to her chest. Nausea threatened. When she tried to call for help, no sound came out. Her body swayed, and she was unable to stop herself. The last thing she remembered was seeing the moldy goblin mound coming for her face before she blacked out.

Chapter Five

"What happened to her?" Dar questioned the nurse as he motioned toward Malina's door. A curtain had been drawn over the glass to give her privacy, but if he was to lean to the right, he might be able to catch a glimpse of her inside. He didn't lean.

"Are you family?" the nurse inquired. "Family is to stay in the waiting room. Someone will update you with any progress. You're not allowed back here."

"Where is here?"

"The Cardiac Care Unit," the nurse answered. "This area has restricted access, and she's not up for visitors yet. The doctor will be out shortly to speak with family members."

"What happened to her?" Dar repeated. He was a little surprised that it had taken so little luck magick to bring the great warlock enchantress down. She must have been taken by surprise if a few ghosts, fairies, and a smelly goblin managed to get to her. The small attack was supposed to be an amusing prelude.

Dar touched the nurse's shoulder, giving her an infusion of luck, which often brought with it a little happiness. It wouldn't last long, but normally it put people in a helpful mood. She stuck her hand in her pocket and pulled out a watch.

"How did...? My grandfather's watch. I've been searching everywhere for this. I thought..." She blinked as if realizing where she was. Her smile was a little more generous when she looked at him. The small haze of his power flowed over her gaze like a reflective sheen. "I'm sorry. What did you say your name was?"

"Darragh Lahey," Dar answered.

"And are you family?"

"I'm her husband. You can tell me everything. What happened to her?" Dar took a small step toward the window. He didn't want to look at her so instead stared at his reflection. He'd gotten a haircut before coming. When the beautician mussed the thick locks into haphazard place, she'd insisted it was a "sexy-as" look for him. He wasn't sure what that meant. Sexy as a what? He absently brushed a dark strand up and away from his face. He straightened his suit jacket with several decisive jerks.

"I'm sorry. I didn't realize she was married. They must have forgotten to put that on her charts." The nurse lowered her voice as if telling a secret. "Your wife had a cardiac event, Mr. Lahey."

Cardiac event? How strange that a powerful supernatural being would end up in a human hospital for something so ordinary.

"What caused it?" he wondered aloud.

"There doesn't seem to be any blockage," the nurse explained, "which is good, but that does lead us to question why this happened. I'm sorry, the doctor should—"

"Will she live?" Dar asked, again briefly placing a lucky hand on the woman.

"I can see that you're worried about her. She's young and strong. We're going to repeat the EKG and draw labs for cardiac enzymes. We'll know more in twenty-four hours. Right now she's comfortable. We have her on oxygen and I.V.

fluids, and we're monitoring her heart." The nurse patted his arm. "I promise we're taking good care of her."

Dar stiffened as he detected a supernatural presence approaching. It was probably the MacGregor family.

The nurse reached for the door, "Do you want to go in for just a second and see—"

"No," he interrupted. She seemed surprised by the suddenness of his response. "Thank you for your kindness. Finding a lost object is a good sign. If I were you, I'd buy yourself a lottery ticket before 4:43 today or that luck may run out."

"Oh, ah," she glanced down to the pocket that had the watch. "Ok. Thank you. I..."

Her words faded as Dar quickly disappeared around a corner and hid in a supply closet where the MacGregors wouldn't discover him. He knew luck would be with him as he waited. Then, when he instinctively felt it would be time, he opened the door and stepped out. He moved back toward Malina's room, keeping close to the wall. No one was at the main desk in the center of the wing. As luck would have it, her door was cracked just enough to let him hear inside.

"How can her heart be bad? That's a human

disease," one of them was saying. By the Scottish accent, he could well deduce it was a MacGregor. The whole clan of them stuck together like... well, like a Highlander clan.

"Not true. One of my ancestors died of a weak heart. If I remember the stories correctly, it had something to do with the type of magick she was casting," another answered. "The spells weakened her over time."

"I thought the legend said Molly died of a broken heart," a man countered. "A spell she cast accidentally killed her lover, and she couldn't take the pain of it."

"One does not die of a broken heart. They only wish they had. Fergus can attest to that," yet another added.

How many MacGregors were there in the hospital room? He tried to peek through the crack. Someone's back blocked Malina from his view. The idea of her in a hospital bed brought him no pleasure. It was not supposed to be this easy to best her. He had hunted her down and planned his revenge in so many ways. One simple haunting would not take away his fun.

"Besides, Malina doesn't fall in love." It was the same voice that had spoken seconds before. "She merely bides her time. I have never seen her give a gentleman caller more than a passing glance."

"Aye, and why should she? The single life has been good to me. I'm happy." The words slurred a little as if the man speaking them had been drinking.

"Right, Raibeart, happy to be single. That's why ya have been proposing to every female that crosses your path—including the two nurses at the reception desk."

"The one I'm meant to be with will say aye," Raibeart explained.

Dar gave his reflection a wry glance. So even her family knew the truth about her. Malina played a sweet game, but in the end, she was as heartless as they came. She took what she wanted, when she wanted it, and she left behind destruction in her wake. She had to be stopped.

"Well, Cait? Can ya help her?" a man asked.

"Aye," Cait answered. "But not here. All of my supplies are currently locked up in the house being held hostage by poltergeists."

"We can get her out of here, but erasing the records of her stay is going to take a little maneuvering." He remembered the voice as being the brother locked in the trunk of his car. "They did a lot of tests on her when she came in. It would be better if she woke up and signed herself out."

"If this is a mortal disease, it might be best if she stays here until she's stabilized. I can help her, but until we know what happened to her, I can't even begin to cure her," Cait said.

"Interesting choice for a hangout, Dar." The smooth voice was unexpected and caused him to stiffen. "Never took you as one to steal luck from the near dead."

Dar pulled away from Malina's door and glanced at Apep. The man was clothed like he'd just come from a catalog shoot for a department store. Slicked back blond hair and green eyes made him look more Nordic than the Egyptian line he was descended of. Even his pose appeared camera ready.

With a dismissing gesture, Dar went to the patient's room next to Malina's. "I could say the same for you. What's a man of chaos doing in a peaceful place like this?"

Dar stopped at the end of the patient's bed and lifted his chart. The man sleeping on the bed didn't move and didn't appear to be doing too well. The bad luck practically oozed from the patient like a dark sludge only Dar could see.

"It's true," Apep admitted. He nudged the sick man's foot aside and sat on the bed. His pant leg lifted to reveal a bright yellow sock on one foot, and a dark red one of the other. Ah, there was the chaos hiding beneath the calm surface. Apep managed to hide himself well, but as a fellow demon his nature always seeped through. "I normally wouldn't be caught dead in Wisconsin. Too many cows and not enough people, but then the strangest thing happened last night. I was enjoying the funniest little catfight between two men who both wanted to be the new face of Zigman Tires when I became all tingly. Before I knew it, I'd booked a flight for Wisconsin, not knowing why. Imagine my surprise to see my old Vegas chum here rousing up some beautiful disorder. I must thank you for the invite. I have to wonder why I'd never heard of Green Vallis before now. It's so... powerful. We're going to have a lot of fun here."

"We?" Dar frowned. He didn't like the sound of that. This was his revenge, and he didn't want to share it.

"I thought we'd get the old pack back together." Apep grinned. He reached for Dar's lapel and gave it a small flip. "Looks like you're still living the glory days, huh? Haven't updated the wardrobe in a few—sixty or so—years." He held up his hands when Dar's expression became defensive. "Oh, hey, I get it. 1950s Las Vegas retro. Wisconsin chicks probably dig it."

Knowing that he was someday going to regret his actions, Dar placed a hand on Apep's arm and the other on the sick man's leg. The chaos demon blinked in surprise and glanced down to where they touched, clearly not expecting Dar to use his powers on him. The dark sludge transferred from one man to the other as he infused his old acquaintance with the sick man's run of bad luck. That turn of fortune would give Apep the opposite of what he desired. Since he desired to stay and get the old demon gang back together, he'd be forced to leave.

"What the hell, man? Not cool!" Apep jerked violently. "So not cool."

Apep disappeared. Dar instantly regretted his actions. Perhaps he'd given the man a little too much bad luck.

The patient took a deep breath and opened his eyes in confusion before his heart monitors began a long, annoying beep. For a second, the man seemed relieved before the life slipped completely out of him. Dar hadn't expected the patient to die, but sometimes luck was unpredictable like that. Good luck for this man was apparently an easy death. Still, he felt a tiny pang or remorse. That's where a lot of humans pegged his kind wrong—sure there were evil ancient demons from the fire realm, but then they'd started calling his people demonic, as well as fairies, and goblins, and any manner of supernaturals. He wasn't evil. If anything he was a demi-demon. He never liked it when his powers resulted in an innocent person's demise.

He detected footsteps coming for the heart alarm and quickly backed out of the room. His foot tripped, and he stumbled into a MacGregor. It was one of the younger men—probably Malina's cousin or brother. The MacGregor held a cell phone to his chest, and leaned to look at where the alarm was going off as nurses rushed past them.

"I'm very sorry for your loss," the MacGregor said in a low, respectful voice.

Dar glanced over his shoulder to the dead man and then nodded. "Thank you. Dad's in a better place now."

"Rory?" a voice bellowed from the phone.

Rory nodded sympathetically as he lifted the device to his ear. "Aye, I heard ya, Uncle Angus. I don't want ya to worry. Malina is in good hands. We'll sort this out, I promise. Ya stay with your wife. Don't interrupt Aunt Margareta's—ah, *treatments*."

Rory disappeared into Malina's hospital room.

Dar backed away, keeping his eyes on Malina's door as he moved down the hallway. Eventually, the warlocks would have to deal with their possessed house and would leave Malina with less of a magickal guard. All he had to do was be patient and wait.

Chapter Six

Malina jerked the needle out of her hand and flung it aside. How was it her family put her in a hospital for mortals? For a moment, she thought it might be a prank. Mischievousness ran in the bloodline and Euann would want payback after she tore apart his car and didn't put it back together again. When she saw the set of brake pads on her stomach, she was sure of it.

"Ha, ha," she croaked before clearing her throat. "Very funny."

Malina gripped the brake pads with one hand as she kicked her legs to free them of the sheets. Bare feet hit the cold tile. She yanked at the various wires stuck to the adhesive pads on her skin. The heart monitor alarm sounded, and she shut it off with a wave of her hand. She stumbled toward the door. Her calf muscles were stiff, and her movements lacked grace.

As she reached for the door frame for support, the soft sound of Dean Martin singing '*Sway*' filled the room. Malina inhaled sharply as a deep pain filled her chest. She dropped the brake pads and pressed her fist over her heart. Gasping, she said, "Turn it off."

"Is that any way to greet the love of your life, darling?" The words could have been anything. It was the voice that further choked the breath from her lungs. The tone rushed over her like the remnants of a nightmare. She looked at her hand seeing blood marring her flesh where the I.V. was yanked from her skin. It pulled a fleeting memory from deep inside her mind, another time when blood had splattered her. The image was gone before she could hold on to it. She felt the human drugs in her system, blurring her thoughts and dulling her reactions.

"No." She pressed her eyes tightly shut and shook her head in denial, willing the ghost to disappear. She remembered the hauntings at MacGregor mansion. There had been so many of them, but she never expected *him* to be one. "Leave me in peace spirit."

His laughter rose over her, piercing the fog of her thoughts. He sounded so angry. "I'm afraid I can't do that. Leaving is your trick, doll face, not mine."

"This is a cruel game, and I will not listen," Malina could barely get the words out. They were nearly inaudible. She again reached forward and placed her hand on the metal frame, ready to leave. "My brothers have gone too far, summoning this delusion. This is only a memory spell that Erik cast as payback for the love potion I tricked him into falling under. He doesn't know what he's done. He didn't know about you. I never told them."

"That hurts, baby," he pretended to act wounded.

"You're dead," she insisted, willing him to leave her. "You're not real. You're not real. You're not—"

"If I'm merely a delusion, then why won't you turn around?" The voice drew closer. It couldn't be him. Not him. "Not that I mind the view through the hospital gown. I see you never got around to having that mark removed."

Malina couldn't be bothered to cover her naked ass. She peered at her feet and dropped her hand from the door. Slowly, she rotated, keeping her eyes down-turned. Her heart beat in painful thuds, and she still found it hard to breathe past the fear building inside her. The dizziness in her brain invited her to black out, and she dearly wanted to accept that invitation into oblivion. Her hands shook violently.

The song didn't stop. The memories it tried to evoke had been long suppressed and locked away. She was now too terrified to look at them again.

Malina's gaze went to where an old handheld cassette player sat on top of the disheveled bedding. She stared at it, willing the device to stop. Her magick caused the song to slow and morph as the cassette tape malfunctioned. Finally, it popped, and the ribbon flowed from inside the recorder.

"That wasn't very nice, doll face."

She saw his feet first—polished shoes and finely tailored suit pants. The delusion was perfect down to every last detail. Hints of strong legs beneath fine fabric were like looking into the past. She knew her eyes would find the slim fit suit jacket and skinny tie. The lapels would be exactly two and a quarter inches wide, measured and cut by hand. The pain became worse as a ruby glinted on a masculine finger.

Her gaze stayed on that hand, knowing that ring. Her family's ring.

Malina was a coward. She couldn't meet the apparition's gaze. "You can't be here. You're dead."

"You won't look me in the eye. You won't say my name. You won't even drop the fake accent." He clicked his tongue. "I think we both know I deserve better than that."

"You're dead, Dar," she countered. "There is no cure for that. You should move on to whatever is waiting for you."

His fingers twitched, and she took an involuntary step away from him. Once they began to move, she couldn't get her legs to stop. She backed her way through the door, still not looking at his face.

"You never believed in luck, did you, doll face, even as you tried to steal all of mine," Dar called after her. "But you will."

She hurried backward down the hall, stumbling as she hit a cart. Her eyes focused on the hospital room door. Dar appeared, holding his broken cassette recorder. He tucked it into his front suit pocket, and she could no longer avoid seeing his face. She panicked and magick blasted from the tip of her finger, shooting a small burst into a nearby outlet. A pop sounded and smoke began to curl up the wall.

In that brief moment, the past came back to her in a magickal wave, unfurling with the smell of smoke. Brown eyes reminded her of a different time when she had been a different woman. The loud blast of horns and drunken laughter came at her in a chaotic rush. More smoke than could be produced by an outlet curled from the hospital floor, bringing with it glimpses of a time long buried.

"Confess," a voice whispered. It was his voice coming out of a locked box in her memory. She thought to feel the tickle of breath on her neck. She had heard him before she'd seen him for the first time and she'd felt his words as if they'd just been spoken. They'd sent a chill through her, low and powerful, setting off her magickal alarms even as it lulled her to the danger it clearly offered. Las Vegas in 1960 had been a wild time, full of wealth, parties, music, and private retreats in the desert. Malina had been in the middle of it all like a movie star minus the movie.

"Confess what?" Malina mouthed what she'd said in the past.

He'd turned her around from the bar to look at him, into those soulful brown eyes, into that handsome face. Cold liquor spilled on her hand, but she didn't care. The chill now crept up her arm as if something so insignificant needed its place in this madness.

"Confess that you know in this very moment you're in love with me," he'd said.

She should have slapped him for touching her arm. She should have run. Instead, she'd kissed him. Even now the pressure of his mouth was imprinted on hers. The smoke cleared from the hospital ward and the drunken party faded. The present took its rightful place as it forced the past back where it belonged.

"I knew tonight was my lucky night," he'd said when the kiss broke. The memory of it echoed one last discharge from her locked memories.

"I don't believe in luck," she said aloud to Dar standing before her.

Just then, the overhead lights glowed brighter and then dimmed before the power suddenly went out. A second passed before the backup generator kicked on. Red lights replaced the white. Dar had vanished.

"Malina?" Euann's voice came from behind. "What are ya doing out of bed? Where are the nurses? Why did ya take out the plug-in?"

"Get me out of here," she demanded. "I don't know what game this is, but I'm not amused."

"Malina, ya should get back in bed. You're very sick." Her brother tried to take her by the arm.

"What is this spell? Was it you because I tore apart your car? Or Erik paying me back for slipping him the love potion? Where did he find such a powerful memory spell? I don't believe in luck, and this is not lucky and..."

Euann shook his head in denial. "Malina, you're not making sense. I need ya to hear me. You're sick. You're *human* sick. The doctors said your heart is weak and—"

"What? Human sickness? Are you listening to yourself? That makes no reasonable sense." Malina took a deep breath, not liking the seriousness of Euann's expression in the eerie glow of the red light. "I don't know what's happening here, but I'm not suffering from a weak heart. If only it were that easy. Someone is bringing back the dead to haunt me, or us, or just me."

The overhead lights flickered as the main power came back on.

"A few ghosts haunting the mansion will be easy enough to deal with," Euann assured her. "They're dead. There is not much they can do. Cait thinks they followed the lost part of Elspeth's spirit when she reentered Donna. Ya know Uncle Fergus isn't the best with his spells."

"They're not just in the mansion." Malina started to lift her hand to her head, only to stop and nod back to her room. "They're here too."

"In the hospital? That would make sense, Malina. This place has seen a lot of death. I guess if I can't convince ya to stay, then I should take ya with me. We broke into Lydia's house and are crashing there. They won't be back from the trade show for at least a week, so the place is empty." Euann gestured for his sister to walk with him as he ushered her from the hospital. Whenever they passed someone, he lifted his hand, magickally blocking them from being noticed. "Da offered to fly back."

"No," Malina said. "He should stay with ma."

"That's what we told him," Euann assured

her. "Cait decided that until we know what's happening, we shouldn't call the others home in case there's a real threat. I don't think there is, but Cait's an elder, and there is no arguing with her on it. She's worried about ya. I told her ya are a strong lassie, even for an English rose."

Malina tried to hold the back of her gown closed as they passed and air vent. Euann stopped to borrow a wheelchair for her. She thought about protesting but knew they'd make faster time with him pushing. He stayed silent as he wheeled her through the lobby out the front door. The snow had melted from the sidewalks, and the warmth of the sun made a peculiar contrast to the slushy white on the grass.

"Where's your car?" Malina asked when they neared the parking lot.

"In a thousand pieces all over the family estate." Euann gave a small laugh as they made their way to a compact car that looked like it would be the last option on a rental lot.

"Are you confident the visions I'm having are not revenge?" Malina asked, hopeful that there might be a better explanation.

"While I appreciate your confidence in me, we both know that I'm not that creative. And I certainly wouldn't evict myself out of my own home." He opened the car door for her. "I worked too hard setting up those protection spells and security cameras to let parasitic ghosts inside to drain every electronic appliance and device I own."

Spirits were notorious for using electrical power to generate the energy they needed to manifest. It's why lights flashed, and televisions became unreliable when they were near.

Malina glanced at the back seat as Euann shut the car door. It was filled with electronics and magazines. "What's all this?"

"Ya all laugh at me, but I'm about to show ya how smart my non-magickal home security is. I'm going to try to tap into the home network so we can see what's happening inside, if there is any juice left in it, that is. If that doesn't work, we'll fly a drone in with a camera. I just need ya to materialize a few things from the magazines once you're up to it."

Malina reached behind her and picked up a magazine. She flipped to a tabbed page as Euann slid into the driver's seat. A woman in a bikini held some gadget. "It's like I told Rory when he asked me to materialize a six-foot puppy. I'm not making you a girlfriend."

A twinge hit her chest, and she gasped the last word, dropping the magazine on the car floor as she doubled over.

"That's it, Malina. I'm taking ya back in. I should never have let ya talk me into—"

"No." Her hand shot out to grab his arm as she leaned up. The pain was still there, but it was manageable. "This isn't a human thing. It's something else. Those doctors can't help me. Only magick can help a supernatural ailment. I need a cauldron, not an I.V. drip."

He appeared doubtful, but finally started the engine and put the car into drive. "I don't understand what's happening to ya, but I will say we're even for one thing."

"Oh yeah? What's that?" She pulled at the hospital gown, making sure it was between her body and the seat.

"I didn't want to see your naked arse either."

Chapter Seven

The sundress Malina found in Lydia's closet wasn't exactly her style, but it was infinitely better than the hospital gown. The tiny flowers on the long skirt and sleeveless halter-top made her look like she belonged in some Southern porch handing out lemonade and sweet tea.

"Ya look like a lady," Cait said in approval, "but ya need a sunhat."

"She needs a sweater," Euann corrected. "It's winter, and she was just in the hospital. She can't leave the house looking like that."

"She's not leaving this house," Cait said. "She's sick."

Cait disappeared into the kitchen and seconds

later the screen door leading to the driveway squeaked open and shut.

"She's a big girl who can make her own decisions," Malina muttered, slightly annoyed by their overprotectiveness. It didn't matter that they were right. She was too tired to leave the house. All she wanted to do was curl up on the couch and sleep.

Erik and Lydia hadn't exactly given them permission to stay at the old Victorian, but they had nowhere else to go. The home was situated on the same hill as MacGregor mansion, just below what the townspeople called the main house.

The Victorian reflected the late Annabelle Barrett, Lydia's grandmother. Malina wondered if that was because the old woman's spirit still haunted the place and didn't want her granddaughter changing things around. Or, if Lydia was just too busy running her business that she didn't think about such things. Malina thought about offering to do it for her sister-in-law as a present. The pink and yellow floral curtains and antique furniture seemed stuck in a time bubble with the only modern addition being the endless rows of body lotions and tea boxes that made up Lydia's inventory and covered every usable surface.

Off the living room, where the family now set

up a base camp to fight the home invaders, were a kitchen and a stairwell. Upstairs consisted of only three bedrooms and a bathroom. Compared to the usual grandeur of the MacGregor mansions, the home was fascinatingly normal. Malina could see why her brother liked living there.

"When did ya do that?" Raibeart scratched his head as if he hadn't noticed her clothes. "Huh, I liked your other dress better."

Rory and Euann snickered and gave her sideways glances.

"The hospital gown?" Malina arched a brow.

"No, that purple one ya had on," Raibeart said. He gestured to his sleeve. "With the things along the thing."

Malina looked at her uncle and then at the Mason jar on the end table close to him. "Found Gramma Annabelle's moonshine stash I see."

"Isn't that why we're here?" Raibeart inquired.

"No, we're ghost hunting," Euann answered, not looking at his uncle.

"Oh, then I'm done. Found one." Raibeart pointed as he fell back onto the couch. He grabbed the moonshine and lifted it in the air. "Nice to see ya, Annabelle." There was a pause before he began to laugh. "Aye, I noticed it was quiet around here. All the ghosts are partying at the mansion. You're welcome to join them, being as it's an undead event." He paused again only to laugh harder. "Ya are a riot, lassie, and a right pretty one too! Hey, so those kids got anything to eat? I'm famished." He stood, mumbling and taking a swig as he went to the kitchen. His voice came from beyond the door. "So, now that ya are dead I'm assuming any previous wedding vows are null and void, and ya are a free woman."

"Did Raibeart just propose to the dead grandma of our sister-in-law?" Euann questioned.

"Could be worse. He could have proposed to the goblin." Rory laughed.

"It's early yet. Give him time," Malina drawled. "If he's distracted with Annabelle, he's staying out of trouble."

"Good call," Euann agreed. "Where's Cait? We're about ready to—"

"Raibeart Donovan Gregory MacGregor," Cait exclaimed loudly. "Remove your tongue from that ghost at once. Ya look like a damn fool kissing the air."

"Cait, we're ready," Malina called.

Cait appeared. "I'm fueled up and ready to go. Hand me that drone."

Rory placed the drone before Cait who began whispering a protection spell to magickally cover it.

Erik kept a portal mirror in the Victorian that led to his mansion bedroom, so the family didn't have to go outside to get from one home to the other. It was this portal that Euann planned to use to fly his remote control drone inside their home to check out what was happening.

"Done," Cait said. "It's as ready as it will ever be."

"Let's hope the protection spell works, and these little buggers don't drain the power from it before we have a chance to see what they're up to." Euann powered up the drone and navigated it to Lydia's bedroom, through the mirror portal, and into Erik's mansion bedroom. Dark wood accented the lightly colored walls of the room, and at first glance, everything appeared normal.

"What's that? Something is hanging from Erik's ceiling." Rory reached to take the drone controls.

Euann elbowed Rory away from him in annoyance and kept flying. The camera angle zoomed past what had been a large painting of Erik in full MacGregor plaid surrounded by the Scottish countryside. Someone, or something, had ripped the canvas down the middle.

"Oh, Erik's not going to like that." Cait shook her head in disappointment. "Such disrespect of our cultural heritage."

Malina wasn't worried about their cultural heritage at the moment. She watched the screen carefully, trying to catch a glimpse of something that would explain why this was happening.

"Why don't we have sound?" Euann asked. "Rory, did ya check it?"

"Aye, I checked it," Rory said, his tone defensive. "Maybe ya have the setting wrong."

Euann reached to punch a few keys on the keyboard. "What power source did ya try to use? They're fried."

The drone turned to show the ceiling. The metal had been speared into the plaster next to the light fixture. "I think that's my drive shaft."

"How the hell did it get up there?" Rory again tried to take the controls and received a hard hand slap in return. "And why?"

"Worry about it later. I need ya go get my cauldron and supplies out of the den, and if ya can't reach those then the spare cauldron in the kitchen," Cait ordered.

Euann used the drone's extendable arm to pull open the door and flew it out of Erik's room.

"Hey, ya started without me," Raibeart complained, joining them.

"How's the future wife?" Rory asked.

"Cait chased her away." Raibeart gave Cait an irritated glare. Cait was unmoved.

"What's happening in the main part of the house? Are they still there?" Malina stared at the silent screen, looking for a glimpse of Dar. Part of her wanted to see him again, even though it would be torture. Another part of her hoped he remained buried. The pain he brought her was unbearable.

Spirits swept past the drone as Euann steered it over the stair rail and then lowered it to the floor of the front hall.

"Aye," Euann answered, stating the obvious. "They're still there."

It was impossible to tell which song the ghosts moved to as they ballroom danced around the MacGregor home. Translucent feet glided in ways that would have been unlikely in their lives. The camera caught a glimpse of the two creepy girls as they stood above the others on the steps, swaying as they watched the performance.

"There, something went into the bathroom," Raibeart pointed at the screen, pushing his finger into the monitor. Whatever he'd been eating left a fine cheesy dust on the display. "Turn the toy. I saw something that wasn't a ghost."

Euann slapped at his uncle's hand before brushing the cheese dust off the monitor. "Hold on. I'm going."

The drone turned sharply, nearly running into the front grill from Euann's dismantled vehicle. He dodged it and started to give Malina a droll look when the screen revealed a rolling tire. Euann jerked up in his seat and moved the controls in an effort to avoid a collision. The drone knocked the tire over, much to the dismay of the three *gremians* who'd been moving it. One of the knobby creatures became trapped under the rubber edge and flailed his limbs. The remaining two didn't bother to help their cohort as they jumped on the drone.

Euann growled and began an animated display of trying to throw off the attackers like a couch-side warrior armed with his video game controller.

"Left, ladies, left!" Raibeart exclaimed, giving a little jump. "We need sound."

"I'm not the one who apparently power surged the internal speakers because he doesn't know how to hook up a computer," Euann returned.

"Damn it. Fine." Rory leaned forward to dig through the computer magazines. He found a picture of laptop speakers and handed it to Malina. She touched the picture and, faster than any 3D printer, the speakers materialized before them.

Rory grabbed the device from the floor and plugged them in. The reverberations of *gremian* screeches were an odd contrast to the dance music the ghosts were playing. Malina stiffened. She reached for Euann's chair back as she wavered on her feet.

"What are they listening to?" Rory frowned. "What's his name? The guy from the Rat Pack."

"Oh, yeah," Euann said, jerking right and then left. He managed to throw one of his passengers off the drone into the stair rail. "Frank—"

"Dean Martin," Malina corrected. She stared at the screen. The ghosts continued to dance in time with the song. Smoke curled out of the computer, and she couldn't move. "'*Sway*'."

"That's right," Rory stated. "Didn't ya hang out with those guys?"

"No," she lied. "Never met them."

"But ya saw them perform, right?" Rory insisted.

"Once. An impromptu performance at a small club," she said, still lying as she added, "It was nothing special."

"I think it would have been cool to see the Rat Pack in all its glory." Rory twisted his hand in the air, and began shouting commands at Euann, "Hit it against the railing!"

"I'm not crashing my drone," Euann rebuffed. He stood from his chair as if the animated movements of his body would somehow help the drone survive. The creepy girls seemed to be the only ghosts watching the drone fly. The dancers were unaware of what was happening beyond their party.

Some of the ghosts stopped dancing and moved to sit at invisible tables to sip imaginary drinks. There was something familiar to the ghost's configuration on the front hall floor.

Malina glanced over her shoulder toward the

kitchen. A chill worked up her spine. She half expected to see Gramma Annabelle's spirit lingering in the entryway. Instead, a light mist drew forward over the floor. The living room began to fade as the past again crept in on the present.

"Confess," a voice from the past whispered. The sound came from the mist.

"Right," Raibeart yelled, jerking Malina's attention back to the screen. "No the other right!"

"Left!" Cait instructed.

The drone flew a dizzying path, creating haphazard patterns in the air. Ghosts became desperate in their haunting, moving feverishly with anger—like atoms colliding in a chaotic universe. The music became a chilling rendition, akin to the soundtrack for a horror movie.

"Confess," the past whispered again so only Malina could hear. The others' eyes were fixed on the screen. She turned back toward the kitchen where the voice seemed to radiate from.

"Confess what?" Malina mouthed, as a tear threatened.

"Confess," it whispered again, this time from the stairs. She understood that the memory was trying to show her something, but she didn't want to know.

Malina shook her head in denial. She didn't want to go back to that night, to that time. She wanted to keep Las Vegas buried deep inside her subconscious.

Malina's body jerked, and she felt herself being pulled toward the stairs. The others didn't appear to notice her departure as she climbed her way toward Lydia and Erik's bedroom and to the gateway mirror.

"Confess," the voice said again, louder than before. The music came from downstairs, punctuated by her family's shouts as they tried to fight off the *gremians*. The mist became smoke, and it curled around her feet, encouraging her forward. A hand reached out from the mirror holding a martini, and she leaned forward to take it.

There was no city as vibrant as Las Vegas in the 1960s—the lights, the loud noises, the chaos of a party that never ended. Music and liquor flowed from every bar and club. Malina recalled the details with vivid clarity—the smell of bourbon, the sound of ice in a glass, laughter from a nearby table, the drunken rhythm of tipsy feet as they moved past her in the crowd. The smoke unfurled from around her feet and moved through the air to meet the end of a cigar.

Malina smiled as she took the glass the bartender placed in front of her. She never paid for drinks. As a beautiful woman in an expensive club, she never had to.

"Confess."

An excitement filled her. She enjoyed a good game. "Confess what?"

The man turned her, spilling her martini. It dotted the skirt of her dark dress, only to hide within the sheen of sparkling overlay material. It didn't matter. She'd been drinking all night, and the world spun in fantastic circles around her. Magick flowed through her veins, and she feared nothing. Why should a warlock fear a room full of mortals, even if some of those mortals were reportedly associated with the mob?

Brown eyes met hers, filling her with excitement. She felt his touch on her arm all the way through her body. His words were light and flirtatious as he said, "Confess that you know in this very moment you're in love with me."

A lady would have protested. When her Scottish parents abandoned her as an infant, English nobility had raised Malina to be a lady. They claimed it was for protection during the witch trials, but that didn't make learning her powers in isolation any easier, and she had a lot to prove. Her wild ancestors' blood flowed wickedly inside her. On a good day that wildness was barely tempered by the antiquated notions of what it meant to be a lady of breeding. Now that madness overrode all else.

She should have slapped him for touching her arm. She should have run. Instead, she kissed him. The pressure on her mouth sent a warm tingle over her flesh. Sexual passion fueled magick, yet this was only a kiss. It shouldn't have made her body swell to life the way it did.

Cigar smoke curled around them from a nearby group. The large red chairs and circular tables were all angled around a stage and dance floor. The club was small and intimate, not like some of the larger hotels. The party became a loud crescendo of laughter and clapping as someone new took the stage. Within seconds musicians played the first chords of, 'Sway'.

"I knew tonight as my lucky night," the stranger said against her lips.

"I don't believe in luck," Malina answered coyly.

"That's a dangerous thing to say in the luckiest city in the world. The Lord of Luck might hear you and take offense." He grinned, an incredibly devilish expression, and she let him lead her through the tables toward the dance floor.

The singer's voice had started before they made it, and the man began dancing her through the aisle as they took the final steps toward their destination.

"Haven't you heard?" Malina flirted. "Luck's a lady, not a man."

His eyes roamed down, and his voice lowered with sexual response. "She sure is. I'm feeling luckier already."

The song was a mere backdrop to the moment. Their bodies spoke on a primal level, anticipating each other's dance moves. Eyes locked. Feet glided. Touches lingered. Onlookers applauded, but she couldn't tell if it was for their dancing or the singer's talent. It didn't matter. Her soul was adrift in time, in a place where nothing mattered. In her hundreds of years, she had never felt anything like it.

The fleeting thought that this was a trick, a spell of some sort, did filter through her mind. She ignored it, not caring. What was the point of anything else now that she had found this second, this feeling, and this dance?

The man said many charming things, gave many tempting looks. He made her laugh with his sharp wit and amusing observations. And by the end of the song, she knew everything in her world had altered. She was in love with a man, and she didn't even know his name. Life would never be the same again.

"Confess," the voice whispered.

Malina blinked rapidly as the fog of the past cleared. It had been so real that she'd forgotten herself. Her feet stumbled to a stop. Her arms were lifted as if to hold a dance partner who wasn't there. She took an unsteady breath as she studied her surroundings.

Las Vegas had disappeared. She was in Green Vallis, Wisconsin, in the mansion's front hall, surrounded by ghosts. The spirits acted out the past for her, an image straight out of her memories. She dropped her arms, seeing the transparent image of someone walking away from her as if leading her past self by the hand out of the club into the Las Vegas night. The music had faded to just a few faint chords of a partial melody.

Escape through the front door would take her

through the thickest part of the haunting. Ghostly eyes were beginning to take note of her presence. Two *gremians* sat at the bottom of the stairs tearing apart Euann's drone. They growled at her as they furiously yanked wires and tossed screws behind them.

"You can hide. You can seek. We won't even try to peek," came an eerie taunt. Malina turned her attention to the two ghost girls looking down at her from over the banister. The children continued, "Naughty girl had her fun. You'll soon regret when he is done."

She ran toward the closest room, a downstairs guest bathroom. There would be a small window she could squeeze through to escape the house. The second she opened the door she was met with a terrible creature. His skin appeared to be red-black char as if he'd just crawled from fire through the bathroom floor. Since he only seemed about halfway through his journey, she wasn't eager to see where the other side of his floor portal led. He opened his mouth to let out a garbled yell as he banged his tarry hand on a fuel tank. Black sludge stuck to the metal, fusing his flesh to Euann's car part.

Malina slammed the door on the bog-man

creature and faced the ghosts beginning to crowd in on her. She ran through them, swinging her arms through the cold spots of their bodies to no avail. With each blast against her skin, she felt them taking her energy. She stumbled into the door frame, weak as she entered the dining room. The goblin had taken up residence on the table, and she gagged as she passed by the stinky den he had built atop the once-beautiful wood. Her shoulder pressed along the wall to help her remain upright.

As she made it into the destroyed kitchen, it was all she could do to open the cabinet to grab Cait's spare cauldron. She rolled the heavy pot out of the doorway onto the back path and tried to drag it over cobblestones toward the garden.

The area surrounding the back gardens looked like a pocket of spring in winter. Dew covered plants that should have been dormant. She fell to her knees, weakly crawling the quickest route out of the English gardens toward Lydia's house. The path was warm but damp from a recent rain.

The bushes rustled seconds before hard thuds sounded. "Me gold. Me gold. She takes me lucky gold!"

Malina gasped as someone jerked the cauldron from her. Two leprechauns tried to drag the pot into the bushes they'd leaped out of while two more ran into the garden to gather golden nuggets littering the ground like rocks. Their brown tunics hung on their thin frames as if they spent more time caressing rocks than bothering to eat. Curly red hair sprouted over their heads in tangled messes growing around to create equally matted beards.

A heavy thud sounded and then another. She flinched thinking they were throwing stones at her. She grabbed a rock and moved to return fire when something struck her shoulder from above. It forced her to drop the rock. She looked up to see a long rainbow overhead raining chunks of gold nuggets.

The sky was literally raining gold.

"What in the ever loving inferno is going on here?" Niall growled, swatting his hands to bat away the falling gold as he approached Malina.

"Bloody hell!" she gasped as another nugget pelted her back. She tried to move, but the ghosts had weakened her body and her magick when she passed through them.

"Me gold," a leprechaun screeched, hopping on her back to get the one that had hit her. He tried to bite her through her shirt. Niall kicked her attacker and sent him flying.

"Stop whining and get up," Niall ordered. He pulled at her arm. Malina wobbled to her feet, the irritation giving her enough strength to glare at him. "That's better. For a second I thought all the fight was gone, and ya wanted me to leave ya here to die."

Her brother looked worn as if he'd been up for days hunting supernatural threats. The thread-bare tartan of his kilt and the hole in his t-shirt attested to his usual lack of priority in the fashion department, though today was even worse. Normally, he was at least clean. Now there were smudges of suspicious goo and dirt covering his torso. She opened her mouth, but no quip came out as her mind drew a blank.

For a second it looked as if he might try to make her run. Instead, he kneeled and pressed his shoulder into her stomach, lifting her up in one swift movement. Niall braced her with one arm as he pulled a handheld crossbow from the other. He shot at a greedy leprechaun who tried to stop them. The arrow lodged in the creature's chest, and she saw the bouncy vision of the leprechaun leaning back over to scoop up gold before disappearing in a puff of green ash.

Her body jolted as Niall adjusted her weight. He brought her to the edge of the spring weather. She was too weak to protest. Niall leaned to dodge a projectile fired at them. As her vision shifted, she thought to see a figure standing leisurely by a shrub.

Dar watched them. His dark suit jacket carelessly tossed over his shoulder. The tingling warning came back to her arm. Was this the beginning of another heart attack? The glimpse of him was so brief she couldn't be sure. When she pushed up for a better look, Niall headed into snowy winter toward the front of the house. Flakes obscured her vision as they traveled into a storm.

Chapter Eight

Leprechauns? Well, that was a new one, even for him. Dar's magick had never summoned leprechauns before. Then again, he'd never stored so much luck and set it out to attack anyone with it either.

Dar had been seconds away from rushing the foul, greedy creatures before Niall appeared. The idea of Malina dying at the hands of leprechauns, or stoned to death by falling gold, brought him no pleasure. This was not one of the many ways he'd pictured his revenge.

Niall carried his sister around the side of the house. This was not the first time he'd crossed paths with the hunter-warlock. It would seem the man was always coming to her rescue.

It was just as well Niall was here too. Now he had both of them in the same location. Perhaps it was time to take his game to the next level. Niall was a hunter, used to taking on any manner of supernatural threat. Mere ghosts and goblins wouldn't scare him. Dar doubted anything paranormal would scare a man like Niall. No, the warlock's fear would come from something quite normal—the fear of losing his family.

Frowning, Dar watched the leprechauns scurry around to pluck gold form the earth to put in their cauldron. He stepped toward them. They glanced at him suspiciously but didn't stop in their task.

"How about a little luck, lads, to help you along?" Dar asked. They smiled at him, baring pointy teeth and making soft growls, as he lightly touched their heads. When he'd gotten all of them, he stepped out of the way.

Suddenly, giant boulders fell from the sky, landing on each and every one of the ugly beings. They puffed into tiny green clouds as he sent them back to the fairy realm where they belonged. Their cauldrons disappeared with them, taking whatever gold they managed to stuff inside.

"Greedy bastards," Dar muttered, as he

watched the rainbow portal disappear. "Didn't even bother to ask if I was offering good or bad luck."

Snow began to fall over the garden, changing the ambient light from yellow to blue. With the rainbow gone, spring was no more. He glanced over the mansion. The estate was just another testament to the power and wealth of the MacGregor family. They had properties all over the world. Yet, the first time he'd seen Malina he had no idea who she was, no idea she was a warlock casting a spell over him.

He should have suspected what she was by the way every man in the room had stared at her. Every gesture had been a dance. And her voice. Oh, her voice. The very sound of it was a siren's melody. He'd watched her from the shadows the second she'd walked into the Las Vegas club. Men were drawn to her, just as he'd been drawn to her. Other women paled in her presence. The only explanation was that she'd bewitched them all with a spell.

Perhaps in that first word, his subconscious had been trying to warn him that she would be his death. "Confess."

"*Confess what?*"

Yep, a damned siren's song. Those two words and he'd been lost. Even now he found himself slipping on his suit jacket to walk after her through the snow. He wanted to make sure she survived the attack.

"Come inside. A place to hide where they will never find you," the girl spirits welcomed him in their singsong voices. They stood in the doorway as if too afraid to leave their new home. One waved at him, urging him indoors. Their eyes flashed with white before again filling in with color. "It's safe in here, so have no fear. It's full of magick residue."

Dar turned toward the hellion children, stopping his pursuit of Malina. He walked into the house, stepping over the shattered remnants of what were once kitchen appliances. Knives and forks stuck into the walls. He thrummed the end of a couple of forks, making them vibrate. One loosened and clanged onto the floor. "I like what the poltergeists have done with the place."

The two girls smiled brightly.

The smelly houseguest taking up residence in the dining room was another story. He was almost sorry he'd given that nasty creature any luck. Flies swarmed over the goblin mound as if what lay inside was dead and rotting. The sound of snores came from within. Random car parts were lodged to give structure to his dung heap walls. Luckily for the ghosts, they couldn't smell their roommate.

Bits of wire and more car parts were strewn over the front hall and stairs. He could well but imagine the same would be true for the rest of the home. A bottle of liquor had tipped over in the corner. Drunken fairies were passed out in the sticky substance, dispersed spasmodically like insects on flypaper.

Seeing movement, Dar held up his hands in defense as he turned. A chandelier crashed onto the floor, spreading shards of crystals around his feet. He slowly lowered his hands and looked up to see *gremians* swinging on the wires that had once supplied the large light fixture. They cackled gleefully at the mess they'd made.

"Such a pity," he said to no one in particular. This had been a lovely home.

His eyes automatically turned in the direction he'd seen Malina in the window. He was drawn to be close to her. He hated himself for it, and yet he found himself going up the stairs and opening her bedroom door.

"Out," he commanded a couple of poltergeists

flying around with her clothing. They looked at him as if they would protest but the two girls appeared by his side, and the ghostly fashionistas instantly disappeared. Malina's dresses fluttered to the ground. He resisted the urge to touch them.

In a flash, the girls were gone. The door slammed shut by the power of an invisible force. The room smelled of her perfume. It wasn't the exact kind she'd worn when they were together, but it had the same fruitful notes.

Dar crossed to the window he'd seen her stare out of. He peered down at the large oak in the front lawn. Lightly touching the windowpane where her finger had traced the heart, he imagined it was her flesh.

Malina appeared near the tree with her brother, and the sight of her shook him from his reality. Snow drifted to the ground but did not obscure Dar's view. Niall set Malina on her feet, and she swayed back and forth. The man grabbed her arm to steady her.

"Confess," he said, though she couldn't hear him. His breath fogged the windowpane. "Confess that you know in this very moment you're in love with me." The glass cracked beneath his fingers as she looked up at him. He dropped his hand. "Only this time, make the confession be true."

Chapter Nine

"Lydia is not going to be happy that *gremians* found their way through the portal mirror into her home," Euann's voice came from the darkness. "And when Lydia's not happy, Erik gets grumpy. When Erik gets grumpy... well, actually, it's kind of funny so I'm not too worried."

Malina tried to open her eyes. Her lids felt heavy.

"Let's hope that spell we cast keeps them contained in the house," Rory answered.

"This reminds me of the time I got a rash. Spread like wildfire on dry branches," Raibeart offered to the conversation. "Nasty thing."

"The rash or the woman who gave it to ya?" Rory teased.

"Hey now, I deserve a little respect," Raibeart began in protest, only to add, "but come to think about it, both."

Euann and Rory laughed. Malina blinked heavily trying to lift the fog blanketing her mind.

"She's awake," Niall stated as if he'd been watching her for signs of life. He sat on a wooden chair next to the couch. His rigid body looked prepared for battle. She met her brother's serious expression and knew the questions he wanted to ask before he even spoke. He leaned closer. "Did I see who I think I saw?"

Malina pushed up from the couch and glanced around Niall's downtown Green Vallis apartment before nodding in the affirmative. The fact that he had a couch was only because Malina had the place decorated. Otherwise, Niall would be using a mat on an empty floor. He was barely there long enough to call the place home. He wasn't the only family member to find a residence away from the mansion. MacGregors had taken up residence around town. One thing was for certain. Since the early days in the wild Scottish countryside, her family kept close.

Euann, Rory, and Raibeart sat at a table with a deck of cards and a half-eaten pepperoni pizza.

Euann held up a slice. "Hungry? Niall has beer in the fridge."

Malina shook her head in denial. "What happened?"

"Ya tried to take on the ghost army yourself, and they drained ya dry. *Gremians* saw ya pass through the portal. They invaded Lydia's house," Rory said. "There is lotion everywhere. Gramma Annabelle is pissed, according to Raibeart, but he also says she is sweet on him."

"She is," Raibeart insisted. "Even the dead ones can't resist my many charms."

"Also, I think ya got goblin dung on ya cause ya smelled awful. Cait had to clean ya up and change your clothes," Euann added. "I don't think I'm getting my rental deposit back, so that's two cars you've now ruined for me."

Malina gazed down to the baggy sweat pants and t-shirt that clearly belonged to one of her brothers. The t-shirt's faded writing boasted the best tacos in the Midwest. Seeing the small hole in the thigh, she could well guess which brother. Niall.

"Then leprechauns dropped out of the sky," Rory said.

"This doesn't make sense. Leprechauns and

goblins, fairies and ghosts," Raibeart mumbled, frowning at the cards in his hand as he rearranged them.

"Don't forget the *gremians*." Rory set his cards down and reached for a slice. He made a great show of lowering the tip into his mouth.

"And some kind of tar creature or bog person," Malina put forth, adding to the strange list. "I saw it in the bathroom pawing Euann's muffler."

"What the hell were ya thinking of going in there alone?" Euann didn't glance up from his hand. He threw a couple of cards on the table. "Hit me."

"I wasn't." It was true. Malina vaguely remembered following the cigar smoke through the portal. What had become abundantly clear was the dance, the eyes looking into hers, the memory of how she felt. Decades of suppression did nothing in the light of a recalled touch. Longing filled her, causing her to ache all over. Her arm tingled, and she stretched her fingers. The overwhelming emotion made it hard to concentrate on figuring out what to do about the attacks.

"I can't hit ya, we're playing that number matching game," Rory denied. "Give me your sevens."

"I can hit him," Raibeart leaned up and punched Euann on the shoulder with a loud smack. "And I thought we were playing Gin Rummy."

"Ow, stop it. We're playing poker, and ya know it," Euann grumbled, making a show of rubbing his arm. He turned to direct his stare at his sister. "Damn straight ya weren't thinking, Malina. I should hit ya upside the head for that. Or worse, I should call and tell ma on ya."

"Kiss up," Malina muttered. "Leave ma alone."

Niall touched Malina's arm and gave her an insistent stare. "Did ya?"

Malina shook her head in denial. "I didn't do it."

"How?" Niall insisted.

"I don't know," Malina said, trying to keep her voice low.

"But, it is?" Niall clarified.

"Aye." Malina nodded. "It is."

"Ya spoke to him?" Niall leaned closer, a deep frown furrowing his already stoic brow. His eyes glared at her as if he could force a different answer because the truth of the matter boded ill for everyone.

"Aye." She nodded.

"What are the two of ya going on about?" Euann demanded. He threw his card down and declared, "I win," before turning his attention to Niall and Malina.

"Whatever," Rory dismissed, also tossing down his cards.

"Damn it," Raibeart grumbled. "I was so close."

"Ya owe me a hundred dollars," Euann told Raibeart.

"I do?" Raibeart asked in surprise. He patted down his chest as if to materialize the money. "I don't even remember betting. I'll have to get it to ya later. I'm a little light after the seductress stole my wallet this morning."

"Malina." Niall forced her eyes back to his, and away from the confused card game. "What did he say?"

"What are ya talking about?" Euann stood and crossed over to them. "Why do I get the impression ya two know what's going on here?"

Malina looked at Niall and slightly shook her head. He'd sworn never to tell, and she desperately wanted to hold him to that promise. Niall's serious expression didn't change. She shook her head again. His eyes narrowed ever so slightly. Malina sighed.

"This is my fault. His name is Darragh Lahey, and he's a—*for lack of a better term*—a luck demon." Malina bit her lip, not wanting to say more. If only her family could let it go with that simple explanation.

"A luck demon? Like that Irish clan from way, way back in the day?" Rory questioned. "I didn't even know those things were around anymore. I thought they died out long ago."

"Aye, he's real," Niall said. "Malina and I trapped him in Vegas and took care of it."

"I guess that makes sense if he thrives off luck. What better city than Las Vegas? I remember people accusing each other of using one when we used to go to Dublin's gaming halls. Damn, that'd be awesome to have a guaranteed Las Vegas lucky streak. So, what's the big deal? He just feeds off gamblers and takes their luck or something?" Euann asked.

"Essentially, aye. Dar can give and take both good and bad luck. He's pissed about what I did in Vegas," she admitted. "And apparently, he's decided to mess with me."

"I heard they look like little sprites," Euann said. "Is that true?"

"No, they're like luck dragons," Rory corrected. "Right, Malina?"

"Ya went around Vegas with a dragon? Or was it a dragon-shifter?" Euann studied her, the boyish light in his eyes excited over the idea of seeing a real, live dragon.

"He's not a dragon or a sprite. He looks like a man." Malina took a deep breath. *A very attractive, charming man.*

"An evil man," Niall clarified.

"Wait, did ya have a gambling problem in Vegas? Is that why ya won't go back or talk about it?" Rory asked Malina. "Ya got into trouble and had to deal with a luck demon?"

"Nothing to be ashamed of, lassie. We've all been there a time or two," Raibeart comforted. "Made a few bad wagers myself." He glanced at Euann. "Even a few I don't remember making."

Niall regarded her expectantly.

"Sure," she said. "I made a few questionable decisions. And now they're coming back to haunt me. Literally."

Niall frowned. It was not the exact truth he wanted her to tell. She didn't care.

"Anyway, Dar was killed, and now he's found a way to haunt me. It looks like he invited a few friends too." Malina stood, trying to hide her nervousness as she walked to the fridge. "Someone said something about beer?"

"That can't be, lassie. Those that the humans classified as demi-demons don't come back as ghosts. If anything, ya might have separated him from his mortal coil for a spell, but I guarantee he'd not be floating around in the ether for long. If ya truly killed him, he would not be showing up now." Raibeart said. "Now hand me one of those beers."

"Ya had enough," Euann denied their uncle on Malina's behalf.

"Ach!" Raibeart gestured in dismissal.

Niall's fridge was bare except for a couple of six packs of cheap beer. She grabbed a bottle and circled her finger lightly over the top to magickally unscrew the metal cap.

"Warlocks, demi-demons," Rory said. "Humans are always trying to give us labels and make us out to be evil bastards bent on destroying everything. If they only knew how many times we saved their asses."

"Demons earned their label," Niall asserted in a low tone. "Do not lump that breed in with ours."

"Don't talk to me about what the humans do," Raibeart said, his voice loud as if he was about to launch into one of his long-winded stories. "Ya were not around when they hunted us to near extinction, or the witch trials when they murdered hundreds including your poor Aunt Elspeth. I remember this time when I—"

"Actually," Malina cut him off before he could get started on a rambling tale of his own awesomeness, "I was there when that happened to Aunt Elspeth since she died protecting me from witch hunters."

Raibeart waved a hand. "But ya don't remember it because ya were a babe."

"Aye, true," she said, mimicking the loud burr of his accent. "But ya don't remember last Tuesday. Doesn't mean ya weren't there."

"Not true. Last Tuesday I drank at the bar with royals." Raibeart stood and grabbed the beer from her hand. "I'll take that. Thank ya verra much."

"It does not count as royalty if ya dubbed yourself king of something," Rory teased.

"Or just because someone was wearing a plastic crown," Euann added.

Malina ignored their continued banter as she crossed to peer out the window. If what Raibeart said about demi-demons was true, Dar wasn't dead. But she'd been so sure. She'd seen his body. If he wasn't dead, that meant he'd *really* been at the hospital, not just in spirit form. In no reality could that be a good thing.

Dusk caressed the red brick-lined streets. Green Vallis had an Americana small town charm, one of closely set buildings and potted trees. Downtown's decorations were changed with the seasons, the same wood Christmas wreaths, giant plastic Easter eggs, and Spring Festival banners going up and down year after year. The townsfolk liked football and parades. They walked to the park with their kids and to the post office with their mail. They waved as they drove past each other on the streets. It was nothing like Vegas. A few football bets and lottery tickets wouldn't tempt a luck demon. This was no coincidence that Dar had come.

"I can't do this again. Please don't make me," she whispered, not sure with whom she pleaded. Forgotten memories scratched at the corners of her mind, begging to be recalled. Each glimpse brought with it more emotion than she could process.

"Malina." Suddenly Niall was standing beside her.

"This can't be happening." She saw someone walking in the distance and held her breath until the figure came nearer. It was a woman and her poodle.

"I won't let him harm ya," Niall assured her. "We will not fail again. I'm not sure what went wrong last time. I did everything I was taught."

"Do you remember what happened?" Malina asked, studying Niall's expression.

He nodded. "Aye. Everything. Don't ya by now?"

"No. Not completely. The memories are there, not erased, but locked tightly away like you promised me you would." She touched Niall's arm. "It must have been horrible if I asked you to do that to my mind, and I'm too afraid to pry for details. I don't think I want to see what's in there. But, what I need to know is..."

"Anything," Niall said.

"Is he truly evil? We know for sure? We had proof? He hurts people. He deserves..." Her voice choked as she recalled seeing Dar looking at her from the trunk of a car. The more she tried not to remember, the harder the images sought to be seen. The woman with the dog turned a corner, leaving the street empty except for a couple of parked cars.

"Ya saw for yourself," Niall assured her. "Ya wanted proof and ya bid me to wait. Do ya remember the shooting in the casino? All those people Dar—"

"Stop," Malina commanded, overcome with intense guilt. If she demanded they wait and then people died because of it, she'd be to blame. That would be reason enough to lock those memories away. Who could live with something so awful? Sorrow churned throughout her entire body. She desperately needed Niall to stop talking.

There was one indisputable fact she knew for sure—she couldn't go through it again. Not again. She couldn't live through the pain of watching. It had taken her years and magickal spells to move past the memories, which now waiting for the magick lock to burst open. She was too afraid to look inside.

"Ya were never crowned a Scottish king, Uncle Raibeart," Euann argued from the card table. "So ya can't claim royal rights with the local women."

"The ladies don't protest," Raibeart bragged.

"I'm done having this conversation," Euann dismissed.

"Whoa, hold on a minute. Malina, are ya," Rory stood and forced her to face him, "crying?"

Malina wiped the single tear from her cheek. "No."

"She's worried," Niall stated. He gave the other three men a stern expression as if to scold them for goofing off. "As we all should be."

"Aw, what's to worry about?" Euann said dismissively. It was his way of comforting his sister. He put his arm around Malina's shoulders. "He's a luck demon, and I don't believe in luck."

"You should," Malina countered. "The right string of bad luck could kill every one of us. It could kill everyone in this town."

Loud knocks sounded on the door. They all tensed and turned in unison. When no one answered, the pounding became louder. "Hey, slumlord, I know you're in there! I saw your motorcycle outside, and I'm not leaving until you talk to me."

"Oh, crap, I don't know which lassie that is,

but tell her I'm not here," Raibeart entreated as he ran to hide in the bathroom, clearly thinking the woman screaming was for him. The others didn't pay their uncle much mind.

Malina studied Niall who didn't move. He actually appeared worried and gave no indication that he was going to answer the woman.

"Is that Charlotte?" Euann asked, going for the door. "Dammit, Niall, what did ya do to her now?"

"Don't propose," Rory blurted, going after Euann. "Seriously, you're not in love with her. Don't make me lock ya in a trunk again."

"Shut up," Euann grumbled before opening the door. He gave a wide smile as he said, "Hello, love. I was just thinking about ya."

"Oh, ah, hey, Euann. Is your brother here?" Charlotte asked. Her naturally brown hair had been colored red and was piled on the top of her head in a messy bun. Her jeans and flannel shirt were wet as if she'd been kneeling down to clean.

The woman was pretty, with the kind of perfect skin most ladies would kill for. Ever since her supernatural ordeal and subsequent memory erasing, her eyes had taken on a kind of wild sheen. They darted around suspiciously like a feral cat that trusted no one.

"I like what you've done with your hair," Euann answered instead. "Fiery!"

"Uh, thanks." Charlotte pushed a wayward strand way from her face with the back of her hand. It instantly fell back down. "Where's that slumlord brother of yours?"

"Hello, Charlotte," Niall answered in an even, dry tone. "What can I do for ya?"

Charlotte's eyes met Niall's, and she frowned. "The point of having a phone number to leave messages on is to actually check the messages so your tenants can get ahold of you when shit goes wrong in your crappy building."

"This is not a slum. I live here, too," Niall defended his apartment.

"I've been calling for a month. That makes you a slumlord." She glanced around his home.

"What can I do for ya, Charlotte?" Niall repeated. "I'm a little busy tonight."

"Oh, let's see. You can fix the drain pipe in my ceiling that you promised was taken care of before I drown. You can tell the people in the apartment above me to stop running their dishwasher until it's fixed because they keep telling me they're not but I can hear it, and I get flooded with their dirty dishwater through my bedroom ceiling light fixture. I can't keep up with the buckets when I'm working the two jobs I have to have to pay for this overpriced place. And you can replace my mattress because it's ruined. And you can pay for the chiropractor visit I'm going to need after sleeping on a lumpy couch for too much longer."

"I promise it will be taken care of first thing tomorrow," Niall answered calmly. "Anything else?"

His tone only seemed to aggravate Charlotte more. "I swear, I don't know how you are related to my best friend's husband." She began to leave only to stop. "Yeah, there *is* another thing. Fix the security on the front and back entrances. I don't need gangster looking guys at my door asking questions about you. If you are in deep with a bookie, then that's your business. I don't want that nonsense coming at me. I have enough to do." She paused and glanced at the other MacGregors standing in the apartment. "It's great seeing you all again. Have a nice night."

Charlotte pulled the door shut before anyone could speak.

"Gangsters? What the—" Euann began.

The door opened two seconds later. It was still Charlotte. "Speaking of bookies, here is Mr. 1950s Mobster now." She called down the hall. "Don't bother knocking at my door again. He's in here."

Malina shared a look with Niall, and in unison, they said, "Dar."

"Charlotte, get away from the door." Niall shot forward and grabbed the woman before she could leave. She screamed in startlement and flailed her arms. Niall pushed her so she landed behind him on the couch. "Stay there."

Malina ran for the door to slam it shut, but couldn't stop herself from looking. That extra second of curiosity cost her. It was true. He wasn't an apparition or hallucination.

Dar pushed his way in before she could gather her senses from the shock of seeing him again, knowing he was alive. It didn't take much of his strength to knock her out of the way as she stumbled back on weak legs.

Tears filled her eyes, and she had to blink them back to keep them from falling. A tight pain gripped her chest as she gazed at his face. There was no joy in his expression as he stared at her, and there was only sorrow inside her when she looked at him. All the heartache she'd experienced over the years pushed forward in a rush of chaotic emotions—fear, relief, happiness, anger. He was alive. He was there. He was... pissed off.

"No," she whispered, shaking her head. "You were dead. I saw you dead."

Charlotte shoved her way past Niall, not listening to his command to stay back. "Don't touch me!"

"Charlotte, don't." Malina tried to reach for her, but the woman was too fast as she swung her arms to keep from being touched.

"What's wrong, doll face? Don't you want to introduce me to your friends?" Dar bumped into Charlotte as she attempted to move past. The woman stumbled at an awkwardly unlucky angle and hit the door frame. He caught her and patted her on the head. A strange sheen came to the woman's eyes as he infused her with luck. Malina could only assume it was the bad kind.

"Let go of her!" Euann tried to heave himself forward, but both Niall and Malina thrust their magick at him, throwing him back. He smacked the wall hard and slumped to the floor.

"Ya can't," Niall said. "Not while he's touching her. She's too weak. Any more bad luck could kill her."

"Dar, let her go," Malina insisted. "She's human. She has nothing to do with us. She's fragile."

"Human?" Charlotte repeated, confused. "I don't feel well."

"Just a bit of bad luck," Dar said. "It would appear I have extra tonight."

"Reverse it," Niall said, holding out his bare arm for Dar to touch. "Ya don't want her. Ya want us. Take me instead."

"Is she gone? I'm sorry I'm such a ladies' magnet. They can't seem to stay away from me." Raibeart came from the bathroom wearing Niall's robe. His bare legs poked out from under the bottom hem. He frowned to see the new gathering in the small living room. "Oh, it's only crazy Charlotte. And who's this fella with her?"

"Don't call her that," Euann said from where he still lay against the wall trying to catch his breath. "She's not crazy.

"Lad, when you've had your brains swirled, and your memories plucked as much as that lassie has, ya can't help but be crazy," Raibeart countered. "Now get your arse up at meet Charlotte's new beau. That's no way to greet company."

Dar eyed Charlotte. A trail of blood came

from her nose. "What are you? You're not one of them, that much is clear."

"Please, help me. I have blackouts and seizures. I need to get to the hospital." Charlotte swayed and gripped his arm.

"Seizures?" Niall demanded in concern. "Since when?"

"She is full human, isn't she," Dar said in surprise.

"So, you're still messing with people's lives. What the hell did you do to this one? I barely touched her which means she was unbalanced to begin with." Dar went from restraining Charlotte to holding her up protectively. He backed out of the apartment into the hallway. "But you must care about her if you're so worried about what I'll do to her. Does she have something of value in her memories that you want? Been digging around in there, have you?"

Niall and Malina both made a move to follow him.

"Dar, you didn't come here for Charlotte." Malina lifted her hand toward him. "You came for me. I'm the one you're mad at."

"You're right about that, doll," he said. "This was not how I'd planned the evening to go. It would seem the ghosts tried to take more good luck than I wanted to give them and left me a little drier than I realized. I should have known those two brats were up to something when they gave me a private bedroom to sleep in."

"What were ya doing in our house?" Rory demanded. "What do ya want?"

"Rory, I need ya to keep Raibeart out of the way. We got this," Niall ordered.

"Like hell I will," Rory denied. "Ya watch him. I'm not a babysitter."

"Move over, young'uns, let a real cowboy teach ya how to showdown," Raibeart said in a very bad, very drunken Texas accent.

"Shit," Rory swore. She heard him leave to stop Raibeart from helping.

"Your bed is very comfortable, by the way." Dar kept his eyes steadily on hers as if he couldn't look away. "Smells like I remember you."

Malina did not need the image of him in her bed circulating in her thoughts. Even now, she wanted to touch him. Another memory unlocked and she heard laughter, her laughter joined by his. Her vision fogged, and she whispered, "Take it back."

"What?" Dar asked, confused. "Take back

that I was in your pretty little house with your pretty little things? The years have given you more than you deserve."

"Take it back," she repeated just as she had in the past. She saw his eyes and remembered when they were joyous and happy next to her on the bed with silky blue sheets when they were not glaring at her in anger from across the hallway. The complete memory was there, just beyond her grasp, a word on the tip of her tongue that had been lost. "I'm not just a one-week stand. Tell me you love me."

"Your spells won't work this time, warlock," he mocked. The hard tone drew her from the past, and she gasped as her vision cleared into the present. The hallway of apartment doors was not the place to have a mental breakdown, let alone a fight.

"Let her go, demon," Malina returned, strengthening her resolve against the invading past. Those memories were all lies anyway, a mistake she'd buried for a reason. "Can't you see that poor girl's had enough bad luck all on her own? She's got nothing to feed you with." Malina again offered her arm. Her hand tingled, and she knew it was somehow his doing. If he touched her, she might not survive the heart attack threatening her chest. "But I do. As you said, the years have been very kind to me. Give the girl some of my luck and let her go. There is no challenge in killing a human. Let Rory and Euann take care of her. Take me in her place. I give you my word I will walk with you out of this building."

"Malina, no," Niall demanded before saying to Dar, "Take me instead of Charlotte and my sister. I'm the one who dealt the final blow. It was my idea to attack ya."

"Not so final a blow, was it?" Dar laughed, though the sound held no merriment. "But it did hurt like hell trying to crawl back into my charred skin."

The memory of burning flesh crept into her nose, and Malina gagged. Dar used the moment to reach forward and grab her offered arm. She felt him drain part of her essence from her body. Pain stabbed her in the chest like a twisting knife. Her breath caught as she gasped for air.

She had the vague impression of Charlotte being shoved toward Niall. The woman made a surprised noise.

"Dammit, Malina!" her brother swore. "Ya don't have to do this."

Dar jerked her along with him down the hall. It was a strange sensation, being so devoid of energy and magick. One touch and he took all coordination from her. She tried to punch him and missed, hitting a wall. Her fingers cracked, and she yelped in pain. Aiming she tried to slap him. Her feet stumbled, and she nearly twisted her ankle.

"Bad luck's a bitch, isn't it?" Dar taunted.

Niall and Rory ran up behind them. An apartment door opened, and a tenant shoved a chair out into the hall. The two men crashed into the furniture, and then into the tenant, tumbling over in a mass of contorted limbs.

The pain inside Malina became more severe, and she felt her mind edging toward blackness. What seemed like seconds passed but she blinked and found herself on the street being shoved into the passenger seat of a running car.

"So nice of someone to leave me a getaway vehicle," Dar said to no one in particular as he slipped into the driver's seat. He leaned over to grab her seat belt and strapped her in. "You should buckle up, doll face. The fates are not smiling too kindly on you right now. I'd hate for a car to hit your side of the vehicle and send you flying."

He winked at her, and she gave him a soft, confused smile. "Take it back. I'm not just a one-week stand."

"No, doll, you're much worse than a one-night stand. You're a lifetime mistake." Dar put the car into gear and took off speeding down the quiet small town street.

Chapter Ten

Dar tapped his index finger alongside his temple as he stared at Malina on the bed. Some businessman had been called away suddenly, and the room had become available as Dar pulled into the parking lot. The man had left behind a bottle of unopened whiskey. A knock sounded on the door, and Dar frowned as he leaned to pull back the curtain. A delivery boy stood with a couple of pizza boxes.

He opened the door cautiously, eyeing the parking lot behind the kid.

The delivery boy handed a receipt to Dar. "Large pepperoni extra cheese. Breadsticks. Paid online. All I need is a signature."

"Don't mind if I do. I am a bit peckish." Dar

wrote in a sizable tip and scribbled a line across the bottom by way of a signature before handing it back.

"Cool suit, daddy-o." The kid snapped his fingers at pointed at Dar like he was shooting two finger guns.

"I think those threads are a little dated myself," Malina said behind him when he closed the door. He hadn't heard her move. He wasn't worried. Luck was still with him. Besides, it's not like she could trick him twice. He knew what she was this time and wouldn't be falling for her enchantress ways.

"No one asked for your opinion." Dar turned.

Malina sat at the end of the bed staring at him. Dark circles marred the flesh under her eyes as if she'd not slept for days, even though she'd just been passed out. He tried to ignore any concern that stirred inside him. Everything she did was a manipulation, down to each pitiful look and pretty gesture.

"Old suits, bottom shelf whiskey, pizza, and a cheap hotel room. My how things have changed since the glory days." She gave a mocking laugh. "Dumb luck not paying the bills like it used to?"

"This is more than a woman like you

deserves," he quipped in return. Damn, she still made his heart beat faster with just a look. He wanted to kiss her as much as he wanted to scream at her. "Did you think I'd splurge for the honeymoon suite?"

If he didn't know better, he would have thought his words hurt her. She looked away and pretended to study the painted landscape on the wall.

"You can try running if you like," he offered. "Or try hitting me again. I won't lift a hand to stop you."

"No thanks, I'm good." She held up the hand she'd hit against the wall at the apartment building. "I have a feeling my luck has only gotten worse."

He tossed the pizza box on the bed next to her. "Eat something. You look horrible."

"Maybe because someone turned my home into a ghost dance party, my garden into a leprechaun colony, and my dining room into a goblin den," she answered, even as she flipped open the box.

"Leprechauns were a new one for me. I'm glad you liked it." He smiled, knowing the look didn't reach his eyes. All the times he'd thought of revenge, of what he'd say when he had her alone, and now that she was with him none of those words or ideas mattered. Those same feelings he'd had the night they met flowed forward, demanding to be felt. "So Wisconsin. I never took you for a nature girl. I seem to remember you liked the bright lights of the city or was it the fine dining, expensive parties, and easy marks you enjoyed?"

"It's nice here. Peaceful," she admitted, giving a humorless laugh. "Mostly."

"I thought..." His words trailed off. Watching her pluck a pepperoni off a slice and place it in her mouth caused his body to tighten. Her lips closed over her finger and then her thumb, licking the digits clean. "Uh, I thought I'd find you some place like New York or New Orleans in the French Quarter with lots of drunken frat boys on vacation that you could take advantage of and feed off of."

"I'd rather feed off nature. Sex only leads to trouble." She again licked a finger. "Here we have an entire forest to feast upon, not needing to kill a single tree to refuel our powers."

He barely heard what she was talking about. Dar only assumed she knew how seductive she was being. How could she not? Everything about her was made to draw a man in. She repeated the slow pepperoni eating process several times as if she didn't have a care in the world.

"Just eat it like a normal person," he snapped.

Malina arched a brow and lifted the slice to her lips. She bit into with gusto, shaking her head like a wild dog before laughing. With a full mouth, she questioned, "Better?"

No. No, it wasn't better at all. He needed to stop staring at her mouth, and the smear of delicious sauce along the corner of her lips. One lick and he...

"Fucking hell," he swore.

"Date night not going how you planned?" She took another bite, this time it was a little more ladylike. "What *is* your plan, anyway, Dar? Kidnap me? Torture me? Kill me? Make my luck so bad I want to kill myself?"

"From where I'm sitting, I only see one murderer in this room, and it isn't me." He resumed his place on the chair and reached for the whiskey. He twisted the top and took a drink of the liquor. "You're right about one thing. This is rotgut." He set the bottle down. The fire it sent to his belly made the substandard taste worth it.

He would suffer through anything to calm his nerves.

"Attempted murderer," Malina corrected. "You're still here. And can you call it murder when it involves driving a demon into the fires of hell?"

"Do you know what hell is? It's a fire realm. My people are not even from there. I told you when we first met that I was born near the Cliffs of Moher. If you want to send me to whence I came, buy me a plane ticket to Dublin."

"That's pretty vague. There are miles of cliffs in Ireland."

"Would you rather I use the name of a village you've never heard of?" he offered. "Sending a demi-demon back to the fires of hell from which we supposedly sprang makes about as much sense as me sending a warlock there. And for what? Spreading around luck in the city of sin? Were you that pissed off that I didn't tell you what I was? I'd like to remind you, you didn't tell me either. It's not like we did a lot of talking when we met."

Her eyes dipped, and for a moment her strong demeanor wavered. "Did it hurt?"

"Yes." Though a trip to the fire realm was nothing compared to the pain of her betrayal.

"Fine. If not a murderer, what do you call yourself? Death dealer? That's semantics, and you know it. You don't pull the trigger, but you load the gun and help aim it."

"What are you talking about, guns and aiming?" Dar frowned.

"Deny it all you want, but you take luck from people. You turn their gambling sour. You take away a win. You make them miss an important meeting, or a bus, or a chance encounter that would have led to something more. You drain them of their will to live. That is the gun you load. You might not pull the trigger, but you sure as fuck supply the reason. Not to mention the people you send out into the world with such a bad turn they get hit by the busses or robbed or any number of horrible things."

Her assessment of his character was so sure, so succinct in its accusations that he wasn't sure he could ever change her opinion of him. "That's what you think I do?"

"When Niall told me what you were, I didn't want to believe him, so I followed you on your errands. I saw you. That night, I saw you. You walked through that casino touching people, and they'd lose. Some of them lost big. Every single one. Some of them weren't even gambling before you came by. Then you talked to one particular man for several minutes, whispering at him until he became agitated. As you left the building, he grabbed a gun and began shooting. Do you know who he aimed at?"

"Yes." Dar took another drink before twisting on the bottle's cap.

"Everyone you touched with your bad luck. Every. Single. Person."

"And you think I caused that? You think that I wandered down to a casino and thought, 'Hey, do you know what's missing in this sea of pull switches and spinning cherries? A massacre.'"

"I know you did. I saw you touch them and I saw what happened when you left the casino. I begged my brother to wait, to give you a chance, and that is what happened. I couldn't let you live to do it again and again. I..." She averted her eyes and motioned her hand in the air and the pizza box closed. "Just like you turned my family's luck sour these last several days and tried to kill me."

"If I wanted you dead, you'd be dead." He fingered the bottle again, tempted to down the entire contents and hope for oblivion. How could she think so poorly of him?

"You tried. You sent me to the hospital."

Dar normally wasn't one to explain himself or his actions. He felt no remorse for what he'd done with his life. However he couldn't take the way she was looking at him. "I need luck to live, just as you need energy to fuel your magick. Stupid me, I never did clue into why plants were always dying around you until it was way too late."

"We kill plants. You kill people." She slid the pizza box away from her toward the edge of the bed.

He stood and began to pace the room. "How many times do I have to tell you? I don't kill anyone."

"I saw you manipulate that situation."

"Did you bother to follow that casino shooting story after you sent me packing to the netherworld? Did anyone die?"

"No thanks to you. They were shot. One can't walk."

"Did you ever once consider that I gave those people the good luck to live? And that I gave the shooter the bad luck to not kill his targets? That maybe they lost at the gambling tables because that's not the luck they needed?"

Her expression answered for her. She'd never even considered the best in him. Her composure wavered as doubts were planted in her surety. "You manipulate. You did it to me. You touched my arm and convinced me I was in love with you. You wanted to get lucky, so you used your good luck power to get you some."

"Get me some what?"

"Sex, get you some sex," Malina stated in exasperation. "None of it was real."

"Me?" He threw back his head and laughed at the very notion. "I have never needed good luck to get laid. That was all you, baby. Besides, you're one to talk. You cast a spell over me to make me approach you. You bewitched everyone in that club. Don't deny it."

"I do deny it. I don't need spells and magick to get men to want me." Malina appeared insulted, which quickly turned into a pout. She ran her finger over the floral pattern of the comforter. "Take it back."

"What, need me to tell you how beautiful you are? Not hearing it enough from other men?" he asked, partly as an insult, partly as a probe.

"Take it back," she said again, the words soft and teasing. "I'm not just a one-week stand. Tell me you love me. I know you do."

How could she see through his hard exterior like that? How could she know the feelings he tried so hard to kill?

"What?" Dar paced a few more times in agitation, stopping to lean over to get a better view of her face. She didn't meet his eyes.

She stretched slowly over the bed, her side falling to the mattress as she continued to trace her hand over the comforter. "Say it, or I won't ask you to marry me."

He felt the words like a punch in the gut. It was decades ago, but he recalled this very conversation. They'd been in a hotel suite, exhausted from hours spent in bed, and he'd been unable to get enough of her. Every movement, every laugh, had captured him until she was all that mattered. "Stop."

"That's not fair. This was to be my proposal. You can't ask me first." Malina giggled, and her face remained turned as if speaking to a ghost at her side. "I was going to ask you."

"Malina, stop it," he demanded, stalking toward the bed. He didn't like his pain played out for him like a show to be mocked. "This isn't going to work."

"There's something I must tell you first. It's important. It's about my fam—" She sat up on the bed and reached her hand out. "Room service? Leave it. They'll wait. I need to tell you something, Dar."

Dar grabbed her outstretched hand. She blinked several times before turning cloudy eyes toward him. Something was very wrong. She wasn't teasing him. She was entranced.

A trail of blood came from her nose. She furrowed her brow and whispered, "Tell me you love me. I know you do."

"Malina?"

"I won't ask you..."

"Dammit." Panic filled him as he reached to wipe the blood from her nose as it ran over her lips. "Malina, snap out of it."

"I don't believe in luck."

Dar crossed over to the bathroom and filled a plastic cup with cold water. He dipped his fingers in and flicked water on her face to try to shock her out of her transfixed state. When that didn't work, he tossed the full contents of the cup. She gasped and her eyes cleared. She swiped her hands on her wet face. She adjusted her position to kneel on the mattress before him.

"You were—" he began, tossing the cup aside.

Malina didn't let him finish the sentence. Wet, cool lips met his in a savage kiss. Her hands found a hold on his head. Dar couldn't tell if she was trying to pleasure him or punish him, but he didn't care. He'd been a fool to think he could go through with any revenge when it came to her. It would seem the decades apart didn't matter. One kiss and he was hers. Just like the first time.

This would only end badly.

He didn't care. She could kill him a thousand times and a thousand times he'd come back just for this brief moment in her arms. The ache of being without her would eternally drive him to his own destruction. He understood that now. This crazy warlock was his fate.

He could tell himself he wanted revenge. He could tell himself he wanted her dead. He could say he wanted to rip her apart and make her bleed. But, when it came down to it, he belonged to her.

One kiss. That was all it took. One kiss and he was overcome.

She pulled back, breathing hard. "I had forgotten that. I had Niall block the more painful memories. It's not all clear, but enough of the past has come back to me. Oh my goodness, how I loved you. Every time you came into my mind I wanted to be with you. To know you didn't mean it as I did, that was the ultimate cruelty."

"None of those claims matter. You ended it, not I. You led me to my death. What else is there to remember?" It took everything in him to stay upright.

"What did you expect to happen when my family found out? You targeted a MacGregor, and not just a MacGregor, the only daughter. They treat me like I'm a delicate flower who needs protection from every boot on the planet. Did you think the warlocks would roll over and give a demon protection? Did you think it wouldn't matter that you tricked me into loving you? Did you think I could be with a man who causes so much death and pain? And I played into your hand so easily. Like a stupid schoolgirl, I believed everything you said to be real. I thought you wanted me for me, not because of who I am and who my family is."

"Malina, I told you. I didn't kill those people. I didn't make the shooter bring a gun to the casino. I didn't make him crazy. I did all I could. Yes, those people were traumatized, and some of them were hit, but they did live. Do you think I would leave your bed that night to go on a murder spree?"

"You predict the future now?" she said doubtfully.

"No, but I've been around long enough to know who needs an infusion of what kind of luck. And if I'm going to feed off someone's energy, what better place to snack than Vegas?" He shook his head. "You never knew me at all. And I never knew you. Our being together was a mistake. It's a mistake we'll both have to pay for."

"No, please, don't." She held up a shaking hand as a tear slipped over her cheek. "I can't get over you a second time. I didn't get over you the first time. Do whatever it is you came to do, but get it over with. Don't draw it out." She began rubbing her left arm before placing a fist over her chest. "Just leave town before my family finds you. I feel my heart breaking. Your revenge is complete."

Her eyelids fluttered as she felt limp onto the bed. Her hand rested over her heart as she lay at a strange angle.

Dar rushed to her in a panic. He placed his hand over her heart, barely feeling the beats. He touched her neck to look for a pulse. It too was weak.

"All the good luck I have is yours," he said, giving her an infusion, even those reserves he used to keep himself protected. He felt the good flowing out of him as he took in all her bad. She coughed violently, and her eyes opened. "I didn't target you, Malina. I loved you from that first moment. I love you now."

As his down-turned luck would have it, the door burst open before he could say more. Malina's family had found them, and he'd given her the luck she needed to be rescued.

Chapter Eleven

"I told ya I could find her with my shark-like senses," Raibeart declared, pointing at the bed. Dar's weight shifted the mattress as he hurried to his feet to defend himself. "Ach, Malina, looks like we made it just in time to protect your virtue. *En garde*, ya vagabond, ya defiler of women, ya destroyer of houses, ya ghost whisperer!"

Malina blinked heavily, knowing where she was, but still disoriented as she looked from the bed toward Niall and Raibeart. She had a hard time focusing on any one thing for too long. A bruise had begun to form under Niall's left eye where someone had punched him. The worn buttons on the front of the television looked as if they'd been pressed far too many times. Magick threatened to ignite around Raibeart's fingers. The comforter stitching was frayed, disrupting the sewn floral pattern.

"What did ya do to her?" Niall demanded, surging forward.

Malina tried to stand but the muscles in her legs didn't support her weight, and she fell. She opened her mouth to speak, but only a strange croaking noise came out.

Niall's fist connected with Dar, who endeavored to block the blow but was unsuccessful. Niall hit the man a second time and then a third, a fourth. Dar tried to defend himself, but each block, each punch, each duck was off enough to miss its mark. He had bad luck.

"Get him," Raibeart cheered. "He smells like an Irishman!"

"No," Malina managed to eek out. She tried to push up again, this time getting further than before. The numbness was leaving her, and her vision started to clear.

Niall wrapped his hands around Dar's neck and lifted him off the ground. Dar managed to grab Niall's wrists. The contact was enough to force her brother to let go. Niall jerked back as if feeling Dar taking from him.

"Niall, stop. You know you can't touch him." Malina commanded struggling to her feet as her strength returned. What was wrong with her brother? He didn't generally appear so mindless and chaotic in his actions. Regardless of what was going on, she couldn't watch them destroy each other. "Dar, stop it."

"Step away, children," Raibeart ordered. He lifted his hand, a blue orb of magick forming around his fingers. "Never send a lad to do a man's job."

"No, stop it!" Malina threw herself forward to stand between the men. Her magick visibly flared in warning all around her. Dar's luck was a powerful aid, and she knew this was a conflict she'd win—she just wasn't sure which side to fight. The hair around her shoulders lifted with a static charge.

Dar leaned against a wall, breathing hard from his beating. Niall was no lightweight when it came to brawling. Blood dripped from Dar's mouth and he clutched at his stomach. Red droplets stained his white dress shirt. Raibeart and Niall blocked the door. The small hotel room felt crowded.

"Och, Niall, what's with your sister? Where'd

she get that boost from?" Raibeart glanced around before settling his eyes briefly on the liquor bottle as if answering his own question.

"Just stop it. All of you," she commanded.

"Remind me, laddie, what manner of creature did ya say we are fighting again?" Raibeart whispered a little loudly. "He doesn't look that fierce. Are we interrupting date night? Am I supposed to scare him or kill him?"

"He's a demon," Niall stated loudly. "He's evil. We kill evil."

"He's not evil," Malina protested. "At least I don't think..."

"You're confused," Niall asserted. "That's what happens when you're around him. Ya make bad decisions and mistakes. Ya must not remember, but I do. I need ya to trust me. I'm your blood. I would never lie to ya. We have to do this."

"I've battled demons. He doesn't look like a demon. Well, a demi-demon maybe but those are hardly demon-demons," Raibeart observed. He snorted with a barely contained laugh. "Actually, this dandy looks like a lounge lizard." He lowered his voice and talked out of the side of his mouth. "Is Malina dating a musician from a piano bar? What's his demon power? Putting people to sleep with elevator music? Fashion crimes?"

"I assure you, I've got enough power where I needed it," Dar snapped.

"Oh, aye, lad," Raibeart agreed a little too mockingly. "I can see that. Ya look right fierce for a dandy. Ya took those punches well."

"Demon form doesn't really go with the human décor," Dar adjusted his clothing, pulling at his sleeves to straighten his bloody shirt. He kept a wary eye on Niall. "But I can use it if I have to."

"Take it easy, dandy, I'm only having a bit of fun," Raibeart soothed. "So, demon boy." He made a show of eyeing him up and down. "I've heard of an Irish demon named Valor. That ya?"

"That joker's overrated," Dar quipped. Malina could well guess that he'd be nervous by the magickal firepower in the room, but he was holding his own well. Not many people would stay standing upright after a Niall beating.

"So which one are ya?" Raibeart inquired conversationally. "What have ya done that I'd have heard of?"

"Rail—" Niall tried to interrupt.

"Quiet, and that's an order," Raibeart said.

"I've always told ya, Niall, that ya are too rash to act. We're warlocks. We literally have all the time in the world. I'll not be killing anyone who doesn't deserve it."

"Demons are evil. What more do ya need?" Niall stated.

"Who told ya that nonsense? That's like saying all warlocks are evil, or all strippers want to steal your money," Raibeart dismissed.

"Dar is a luck demon," Malina explained. She glanced at Dar and started to say more, "He—"

"Darragh Lahey." Dar cut her off to speak for himself. He gave a small bow of his head. Just like Raibeart, his tone ridiculed the situation as he played up the role of a harmless dandy. "Lord of Luck. I giveth. I taketh. I'm a good friend to have at the gaming tables."

"Darragh," Raibeart repeated. "Nope never heard of ya, Lord Dandy Luck."

"Well, I've heard enough. This isn't a speed date," Niall interrupted. "Malina, step aside. This is for your own good. He's bewitched ya. Just like last time. I will not fail to protect ya whether ya want me to or not."

"Why don't you let her make up her own mind?" Dar put forth.

"*Thalla gu Taigh na Galla,*" Niall answered. *Go to hell.*

"*Pòg mo thòin,*" Dar answered in perfect Gaelic. *Kiss my ass.*

"I'm not bewitched," Malina interrupted. The power coursing through her veins felt amazing. She felt better than she had in years. Her mind swirled with thoughts, none of them bringing her much clarity at the moment. Wild energy made her want to dance, to sing, to drink, to kiss. She wanted to grab Dar by the shirt collar and drag him to bed. She wanted to drive fast through town screaming at the top of her lungs. Oh, or a bar fight. That would be fun to have a down and dirty brawl in some biker roadhouse. The feelings were amazing like she could conquer the world and make it bend to her desires.

"Ya said that last time too. I know ya, my sister. There is no way you'd let a man that close without his working some kind of spell angle. Look at yourself. That much power is not normal. Now move. I promise we will protect ya. I'll take care of this for ya. I will not fail." Niall tried to push past her, but she held out her hands to force him back without even touching him. Magick twirled from her fingers, urging him to leave. She was tired of this interruption.

"Aye, ya will not fail now that Raibeart MacGregor, King of the Highlands is here—hey, now," Raibeart's tone dropped slightly in disappointment, "why's the demon wearing the MacGregor ring? Those clan rings have been in the family since before Robert the Bruce became King of Scots. What's it doing on an Irishman? He's not a MacGregor, is he? Ya would think I'd remember a demi-demon in the bloodline. Was it Great Aunt Gertrude? She was a wee bit of a wild one. We had a mermaid once, or was it a selkie, or a siren? It might have been a siren. Damn, if I can't keep track of all the relatives. Which family line do ya belong to, laddie?"

"No," Niall interrupted before anyone else could answer. "He's not a MacGregor."

"Then what's he doing with the MacGregor seal?" Raibeart insisted.

Malina's reactions calmed at the question, and she lowered her arms. She gave a guilty glance at her brother and shook her head not wanting him to tell. The uninhabited urges she'd had moments before paled with the reminder of reality. She did have too much power inside her, too much luck. It was making her decisions reckless.

"As a clan elder I demand to know why that man wears our seal," Raibeart placed his hands on his hips. All levity was gone from his tone, and he seemed unusually somber for once. "Ya know that means he's under clan protection. It's a sacred trust. There's no way he could have stolen it. The rings are enchanted and have to be given freely."

"Do ya want to tell him, sis, or do ya want me to?" Niall asked.

Malina shook her head in denial again and frowned her plea for his continued silence. Niall arched a brow and nodded toward Raibeart in an inaudible command to speak.

"Because I gave it to him," Malina said, unable to look at Dar. How was this conversation lucky? His power was supposed to give her luck, not *this*. She felt Dar's presence in the room, and it was more than she could bear. Every part of her wanted to be next to him, to defend her decision. Then again, every part of her also wanted to run away and hide the truth from her family. The stupid English rose pedestal they put her one was a hard burden to overcome.

"And why would ya do a fool hearted thing

like give a MacGregor ring to a demi-demon?" Raibeart demanded.

"May I speak?" Dar asked.

"No," Niall stated a little harshly.

"Malina?" Raibeart said in warning. She'd never seen him so concerned before. "Why did ya give him a ring?"

"Because," Malina whispered to her uncle. There was one truth that was not buried, one she had always known but refused to think about.

"Because why?" Raibeart urged her to finish.

"Because I married him." Malina's arm tingled, and she suddenly knew why. Her body had been trying to tell her consciousness all along. The pain radiated from her ring finger toward her heart. She might have destroyed the wedding band, but her subconscious remembered the pleasure she had in receiving it. It wasn't the piece of metal that her body missed, but everything it represented—a life, hopes, dreams, family, a husband, love. It wasn't some cardiac event. It was heartbreak, and she'd done it to herself. Dar's nearness must have triggered the feelings she'd tried so hard to bury, and those denied feelings were demanding she faced the truth of what she was and what she had done.

Malina managed to look at Dar. His serious eyes fixated on her. The memories of that day were half-formed in her head, but she recalled the pleasure she felt when she joined with him in a small chapel. They'd been more than a little drunk and completely inappropriate by the way they kept kissing as the officiant spoke. She nearly choked on the confession, "He's my husband."

Niall sighed heavily as if a weight was lifted off him. She pouted at her brother though she couldn't hate him for trying to clean up her mess and take care of his family.

"Now I'm confused. How long were ya gone from the apartment? Jeepers, lassie, ya work fast," Raibeart swore. "And why would ya keep your boyfriend a secret? Are ya hiding him from the family because he's a demon, or because he's a little foppish?"

"I didn't marry him tonight," Malina explained. "It was in Las Vegas in 1960 before I knew he was a demon."

"And ya conveniently forgot to mention this at the last thousand family dinners?" Raibeart cringed. "I do not envy ya having to break the news to your ma. I think she's finally going to lock ya in that enchanted tower she's having built like she's been threatening to do for the last decade or so."

"Ma plans to lock me in a tower?" Malina shot in surprise.

"Didn't ya know about that?" Raibeart gave an uncomfortable laugh. "Forget I said anything."

"He tricked her," Niall inserted to get the conversation back on track. "That's what demons do. They deceive."

"Niall, it's not that simple." Malina went to where Dar leaned against the wall. He looked as if it was taking all of his energy to stay upright. "He's not what you think. I was wrong to listen to you last time. You always make me feel like a child who can do nothing right. I was hurt and confused as to why he didn't tell me what he was." She touched Dar's cheek, willing him to take back some the energy he'd given her. She felt him strengthen under her hand. "I'm sorry. I was wrong, wasn't I? I remember things now. Not all of it makes sense yet, but I remember. How can I be mad that you didn't tell me about being a luck demon when I didn't tell you about my being a warlock? Everything happened so fast, didn't it? We made so many quick decisions."

"That doesn't change the fact that he kills

people," Niall said. "Malina, ya know what needs to be done. He needs to be destroyed. Ya might not remember but I—"

"Why does everyone keep saying I kill people?" Dar insisted. "You're starting to make me sound like some kind of mass murdering serial killer."

"That's exactly what ya are," Niall stated.

"Anyone drinking this?" Raibeart reached for the cheap whiskey and unscrewed the cap. He sniffed it before taking a long drink from the bottle. "Ah. Don't mind if I do."

"Ya don't pull the trigger, but ya supply the bullets," Niall insisted.

"Gee, wonder where I've heard that one before?" Dar muttered sarcastically giving a wry glance at Malina. "Not all beings classified as demons by humans are killers. Half of us aren't even demons in the evil way they mean the word. They used to call us luck spirits and leave us little offerings to gain our favor until someone hit the wrong influential lord with a dose of what he deserved and a campaign started against us."

"It might not be what we thought, Niall." Malina motioned that her brother should back up. "No one died during that casino shooting. Maybe we looked at it wrong. Maybe his intervening saved those people."

"Those situations are rare," Dar offered. "Most of the time, I take luck from the undeserving and give it to the worthy. I keep just enough for myself to survive."

"And that man in the hospital room Rory saw ya with? He deserved enough bad luck to kill him?" Niall asked.

"What are you talking about?" Malina frowned. "What man?"

"Ask him. While ya were in the hospital, he was next door killing your neighbor—a guy recovering from surgery who'd done nothing to deserve it." Niall's gaze dared Dar to deny it.

"You really are a Neanderthal. You don't understand anything about luck do you?" Dar slowed his words as if speaking to a child. "Death is not always unlucky. Living is not always lucky. I gave that man a large infusion of good luck. I didn't know it would mean his death, but I can only guess that he was in for a very hard, lonely road if fate chose death as his blessing."

"It is not yours to decide," Niall stated.

"How do you know?" Dar debated. "Maybe it is. I was given my powers for a reason. Maybe that reason is to help those who need it and to take from the real assholes who don't. Maybe it's not yours to judge. Did you ever think about that? Maybe you shouldn't be messing around with people's lives—like that Charlotte. Even I could see she is walking a very thin line of sanity. I barely touched her, and she spiraled—"

Niall tried to throw a ball of magick at Dar, who managed to dodge it by darting to the side. It hit the wall and fizzled.

"—downhill fast," Dar finished.

"How is Charlotte?" Malina felt a little selfish not thinking about the woman until that moment.

"She's with Rory and Euann. We're still trying to figure out what he did to her," Niall stated.

"Ach, don't be so theatrical," Raibeart said between drinks. "She looked better to me than she has in a long time. Ya are just mad because she gave ya that black eye."

"Charlotte did that?" Malina couldn't help the laughter in her tone. "You were bested by a human girl?"

"Raibeart, put the drink down and help me," Niall ordered.

"Ya do realize we can't kill him now even if we wanted to," Raibeart said. "To do so would negate all the protected rings' powers. Those we've given them to over the years would fall to great harm because the pact was broken."

"What are you talking about? They're just family rings," Malina said.

"Ya should pay attention to the old ways, lassie. Ya have a thing or two to learn about your heritage," Raibeart returned.

Malina felt his words like a smack on the face. Just another reminder that she was considered different.

"We did him harm, and nothing came of the ring enchantment," Niall argued.

"Don't remind me," Dar muttered. They ignored him.

"I'm sure it's just a family legend," Niall said.

"Well, maybe that's not one of the enchanted ones." Raibeart gave a small wave of dismissal. "Maybe it was the green stones that were enchanted, and the red ones were cursed? Why are ya asking me about the rings, anyway?"

"I can attest to it being cursed," Dar interjected. "The second it was put on my finger my wife tried to kill me."

"Not the very second," Malina denied. "I forgot how dramatic you could be."

"Fine. That same night," Dar corrected with a hint of irritation. He was clearly starting to feel a little better. "As far as I'm concerned, I'm the injured party here. I didn't expect to spend my honeymoon in a ball of flames and then taking a dirt nap because my wife decided she'd made a mistake."

A twinge of annoyance filled her. That was not how it had happened, and he knew it. She argued, "I didn't expect to be married to a demon."

"Like you have room to talk," he scoffed. "You're a warlock."

"You attacked my home. You sent ghosts," she continued in exasperation.

"You tried to kill me first."

"And goblins, and—"

"You had your brother set me on fire."

"—*gremians*, and fairies, and—"

"Do you know how hard it is regenerate burns?"

"—leprechauns. Who the hell summons leprechauns? What could have possibly made you think that was a good—"

"I'll tell you what's hell. Hell is trying to regenerate burnt flesh. You wouldn't believe the smell. Try walking around like a charbroiled steak for a year and see how you like it." His nearness made her pulse quicken.

"Those little leprechaun bastards tried to stone me," she charged.

"*Hel-lo*," Dar drawled. "You sent me to a fire realm to hang out with full-blooded real demons."

"Aye, those two are married," Raibeart announced with a laugh. "No doubt about it." He motioned toward the bed. "Hey, are ya going to eat the rest of that pizza?"

"We just ate," Niall grumbled.

"Help yourself," Dar offered. His eyes moved between Malina and Niall. She couldn't blame him for not trusting any of them. "I lost my appetite."

"Raibeart, a little help please?" Niall motioned toward his sister.

"Oh, right, welcome to the family, laddie. We like to run bare-arsed in the woods on Tuesdays. You're free to join us if ya can keep up. And, ah, good luck when ya meet your new ma. Thanks for the pizza. If ya get those ghosts out of our house, it will go a long way into helping your case. In this family, we clean up our own messes," Raibeart said.

"Since when?" Malina arched a brow. That last statement wasn't true at all.

Raibeart snickered as he took the pizza box and bottle of whiskey before heading out the door. "Ya coming, Niall?"

Her magick again flared up in warning when Niall didn't immediately leave. Her brother looked as if he wanted to fight her, to demand she listened to him, but she didn't want to hear it. She urged him with a luck-charged power to leave. This time she would not act rashly. She wasn't the same girl she was before.

Raibeart came back to the doorway. "I got it. Red is *djinn*. I never took ya for the control type, Malina."

"What red?" Niall asked in exasperation.

"By order of the MacGregor, I command ya to obey," Raibeart announced in an overly authoritative tone, only to order Dar, "Sing!"

"I'm not singing anything, you crazy ole—" Dar began, only to break instantly into a Dean Martin ballad. Red smoke filtered from the ring up his arm. The further the smoke climbed, the louder and more heartfelt Dar's singing began.

Raibeart swayed his hips and laughed as he danced with the pizza and liquor. "Your dandy's not a bad crooner, Malina." He sang along, only he didn't know the exact words, only the rhythm, so he added, "Bah, bah, bum, bum-bum-bum. Bah, bah, bum..."

"What did you do to him?" Malina gave Dar a little shake. He tried to grab her hands and dip her into a dance move. She barely dodged being swept off her feet.

"Raibeart, stop this at once." Niall's every gesture was filled with frustration.

"Oh, fine, by order of the MacGregor ya can stop now," Raibeart commanded. The singing instantly ended mid-note. "See there, nothing to worry about. Malina has complete control of him. She gave him one of the *djinn* traps."

"By order of the MacGregor I demand ya leave this place at once and never bother us again," Niall said to Dar.

"By order of the MacGregor I demand you don't follow Niall's commands unless you want to," Malina countered. Dar blinked in momentary confusion.

"Dammit, Malina, he's no good for ya," Niall growled. "By order of the Mac—"

"If Malina gave him the ring her orders will always supersede ours," Raibeart said.

"*Djinn*? Like a genie? Three wishes, that kind of thing?" Malina asked her uncle. She'd never been around a genie before.

"I never understood why everyone things ya can only have three. A *djinn* enslavement is an enslavement. It lasts as long as it lasts." Raibeart shrugged. "Now, let's go, Niall. I have this pizza. I'll eat. Ya drive."

"Malina, this conversation isn't over," Niall warned. "I felt ya trying to push me out with your magick. It won't work. I'm not leaving without—"

"Leave them be, Niall, ya are beginning to bore me," Raibeart decreed, "by order of the council of elders. Malina married him there is nothing ya can do about it. But, I think ya know that. It's why ya never told us what ya two had been up to in Vegas. Ya have a lot of accounting to do. We give ya free rein to hunt, but only if ya are full and truly honest about it."

"Ya *give* me?" Niall shot incredulously.

"Aye, laddie, give," Raibeart said. "Now get in the car."

"Malina, promise me ya won't take off that control ring," Niall demanded.

She glanced guiltily at the floor and gave a quick nod of agreement.

Niall pointed at Dar. "Ya are on thin ice, buddy. I'm watching ya. One misstep and I don't care what the elders say. And if ya hurt her..."

"Sounds kinky," Dar taunted with a lazy grin she remembered so well. A hint of who he'd used to be filtered through his expression. It caused an ache in her chest. "You better run. Your elder is calling you."

Niall growled and stormed out of the room. His voice came from outside as he walked away. "Raibeart, this isn't over. The only reason I'm leaving is because of that damn control ring. Just as soon as everyone gets back, I'm convening the elders and overriding your decision."

Chapter Twelve

Malina drew her hand through the air and magickally slammed the hotel door shut behind her brother. In all honesty, she had no idea if she were making the right decision. All she knew is that she had desperately wanted her uncle and brother to leave and they had as if her willing it to happen somehow influenced reality. "I can't believe they left."

"That's luck for you. First, you wanted them to save you, and then you wanted them to leave. I gave you a pretty powerful dose." Dar didn't move from his place near the wall. "That's what they call a lucky break."

"Is Charlotte going to be all right with what you gave her? She's not going to be one of those people who dies because it's luckier than living, will she?" Malina's skin tingled almost to the point of itching. She felt the power inside of her, the longing, the promise of pleasure and the memory of pain.

"If she dies it won't be because of anything I did," Dar assured her. "I'm not the one who scrambled her brains."

"You don't understand. She had witnessed too much. These awful paranormal creatures kidnapped her and attempted to siphon my brother Iain's powers through her body. She was traumatized. We took her memories from her for her own good, and we've been trying to help her ever since."

"Her own good, or to limit your clan's exposure to the human world?" Dar was partially right, and his expression said he knew it.

"Aye, family survival was also a consideration," Malina admitted. "I suppose neither one of us is completely altruistic, are we?"

"So what now?" Dar manipulated the ring, twisting it around his finger. He pulled it off and set it on the dresser near the television. The second he let go, the ring flew right back onto his finger. "I always thought that was because I was holding on to so much anger at your betrayal."

"If it helps, I didn't know what it was when I gave it to you." It had never been her intention to enslave anyone, but now that she had that safeguard against him, she did feel a little more at ease. In a perfect world, there would have been trust between them. Then again, in a perfect world, she wouldn't have attempted to send her husband to hell on their wedding night, and he wouldn't have tried to scare her to death with supernatural creatures fifty-some-odd-years later. Under her breath, she said, "I guess no marriage is perfect."

Dar mistook her comment as he touched his ring finger. "I suppose not. Though I can honestly say, I didn't predict it would include a *djinn* curse. It appears you have all the control in this relationship. So, what now, my liege?"

"Don't be like that," she reprimanded.

"As you wish, doll face," he answered with a mocking bow. It was then she noticed the slight narrowing of his eyes. He looked upset.

"I promise you that I didn't know what the ring did when I gave it to you." Malina insisted. If he was free, he might not stop the attacks on her family. There was a certain amount of safety in having him under her command. She didn't have to assert that control, but it was nice knowing it was there if she needed it. Plus, she did promise Niall that she'd not release him.

"Then undo it," he said. "Free me from it."

Malina averted her gaze. "I don't know how it works. It might take a while to figure it out. It's not like I've ever seen these things in action."

"Command me to take it off, order me free," Dar lifted his ring finger before her face. "Or you take it off."

Malina stared at the stone. A tremor worked its way through her. She started to reach for it, only to stop. "I don't think I can."

"Try."

"First, I need something from you." She took his hand and brought it from before her face to hold it in front of her as she studied his expression. "I need your word that you'll call off the attacks on my family, and you'll get the ghosts, goblin, and all the unexpected guests out of our house."

"If you're going to make me wear it, at least command me to do something fun." Dar's voice dipped meaningfully as he glanced over her body.

"I don't want to command you to do anything." She took a deep breath. "So it is your intention to do harm to my family."

"Honestly, darling, would you believe me if I promised?" Dar laughed. "What's the point of giving you my word if you don't trust me? We both know you don't want me to take it off. But, fine, if you think you need protection from me, then leave it on. I'll not make any bargains with you."

"I would..." Her breathing deepened, and she felt her heartbeat picking up. "I would give you the chance to prove your word."

Dar pulled her hard against his chest. "You are so aggravating. I don't remember you being this frustrating in Vegas. I came here with a clear purpose and now, seeing you again, I'm not sure I can promise I won't attack you or your family if you release me. You see, doll face, I can't make that promise because I don't trust you either."

Confess.

Malina heard the past begging in the back of her mind. When he touched her, it was madness. The rush of emotion surging inside her couldn't be contained. She lifted on her toes and kissed him. Her lips had parted before they met his. Her arms wrapped around his neck to hold him closer.

He felt so familiar as if no time had passed since she'd lain in his arms. Strange how a few short weeks so many years ago could remain embedded in her body's memory. Lovers had come and gone, each a mere passing fling, but with Dar it was different. Her body recognized him—the way his chest pressed into hers, the way his breath caught before he sighed her name, the pressure of his fingers gliding down her back. Each intimate touch was emblazoned on her. This was the feeling she'd been searching for.

Few relationships that were built on something more than the customary—a convergence of mismatched souls that bound together like magnets to defy all logic. Sanity had no place between them. It never had. When they came together, it was instinct and insanity. The feel of flesh was an addiction. A kiss only made the need worse. Release would only make the hunger grow.

Music notes from the past clouded her mind, adding a soundtrack to the rhythm of their bodies. She felt her magick surge as she slowly undressed him. The ache became unbearable. Her hands moved to cup his ass, loving the smooth texture to her palms. Her clothing disappeared by sheer will of her desires. Soon there were no barriers.

The present merged with the past as they made love. The floral comforter transformed into blue silk sheets only to return. Their movements were reminiscent of long ago when they had been in this position. He touched her in the same way as if trying to rekindle the innocent fever they'd had before. The lingering smell of cheap whiskey was replaced by a fine scotch.

Time held no meaning.

Malina gazed into his beautiful eyes. Tears threatened as he drew his arousal along her sex. She felt the power building inside her, a pure, erotic outpouring of magick and luck.

Dar thrust, filling her completely. The room faded and changed around them as if it couldn't decide which memory they belonged in. Gentle lovemaking turned into a feverish need. The present won as their actions became aching and desperate. He pumped his hips hard, driving her into the bed as if he couldn't decide if he was loving her or punishing her. She pressed a hand against the old headboard for leverage, as she clawed at his back, giving as good as he gave.

Climax came in an explosive wave. There was

no secret to hide. He knew what she was. Her magick burst out of her, unable to be contained. The television flashed, flipping through random channels. Lights flickered. The ugly landscape fell from the wall and the dark frame cracked upon hitting the floor. The shower turned on, blasting steam out of the bathroom door. Even the toilet flushed of its own accord.

Breathing hard, he looked around the destroyed room in amazement. "I'm taking it, by your reaction, that it was good for you."

She chuckled, too relaxed to take offense. "Is that you seeking validation?"

"Depends, are you giving it to me?"

"Sex was always something we seemed to get right. We're like two chemical bombs colliding." Malina reached for his cheek and lightly ran her thumb along the corner of his mouth. "I honestly don't know anything at this moment except my legs feel like jelly, and I missed you."

Dar rolled off of her and sat on the bed. He placed his feet on the floor and leaned his elbows on his knees as he braced his head. "What am I doing?"

Malina doubted the question was meant for her. She sat behind him and gently caressed along his spine, moving from his shoulders toward his ass and back up again. "Confess."

"What?" He stiffened.

"That's the first word you said to me. Confess," she said.

"I remember."

"Better late than never, I guess, but here it goes. This is my confession to you. Dar, I'm sorry about what happened. I wish I could take it back. I don't blame you if you hate me. I had so much to prove to my family. I wanted them to see me as a true MacGregor, not just the English rose outcast who'd been sent away and raised by outsiders. When Niall came to me and told me you were using me, I didn't want to believe him even though a lifetime of experiences told me Niall was never wrong when it came to good and evil. So, I demanded proof. Then I saw that shooting, I…" Her voice choked. The numbness in her hand returned, and she rubbed her arm. If she was to give herself another heart attack, then she needed to get her confession out. "I convinced myself that you had to be destroyed, or I wasn't worthy of my warlock heritage. I was angry you lied to me about who you were. I thought you were a demon, that you were evil, that you were using me. I know being a dumbass is no excuse, especially from a woman well over four hundred years old, but there you have it. I was a dumbass still trying to prove something to my brothers and parents. You were the one decision I had made without thought of my Scottish clan, or my reputation, or the desires of my family, and I was embarrassed when I thought that rebellion proved them all right, that I was a foolish chit and you knew who I was along and exploited my weaknesses."

He slowly turned to look at her. She let her fingers drop from his back.

"It turns out they were right about me." Malina sniffed as a tear rolled over her cheek. She didn't bother to hide her nakedness or her emotions. Let him see her vulnerability. He deserved to know everything after what she'd done, and the truth flowed from her in a nearly incoherent wave. "I am a naïve, rash, impetuous screw-up. I tried to murder the one person who wanted me for me—not because I was a MacGregor, or a warlock, or powerful, or had a wealthy family. I didn't trust my instincts when it mattered. I deferred to my brother who meant well but didn't know you like I did. It should have been me convincing him, not the other way around."

"Why did you hide who you were? You were lying to me before your brother came." He didn't move to touch her, but he also didn't pull away.

"I guess I could ask you the same thing, and perhaps some of our reasons would be the same as well. It's difficult to talk about what we are to outsiders." She pushed her hair out of her face and made a small noise of self-reproach. This was to be a confession, not an excuse. "No, it's more than that for me. I didn't tell you who I was because I liked not being seen as a MacGregor. I was just Malina."

His gaze roamed over her features. She couldn't blame him for not trusting her.

"After we..." She hesitated, having a hard time saying the actual words. "Afterward, like a coward, I couldn't even face what I'd done. Instead, I made Niall promise never to mention it to the others, and then I had him lock the most painful of those memories away inside my brain so that you only lived in the edge of my dreams. I knew I had been married, I believed I'd been betrayed, and I knew we had stopped you. I didn't want to forget those facts because I never wanted to be taken advantage of again. What I did forget were the details, and how I felt when I was with you."

"I don't know what you expect me to say."

"You don't have to say anything. I want you to hear me and then do what you will with that. Trust me, don't trust me. Believe me, or don't." She took a deep breath. "As I was saying, afterward, I made myself forget, but only my consciousness. My subconscious remembered. I'd wake up with this feeling I couldn't explain, a tightness in my chest. It was the notion that something was there that I should think about but couldn't quite pin down. It was dread, and longing, and sadness, an inescapable feeling that couldn't be described with words. It was you, Dar. It was the feeling of losing you, of losing what we had. I must have relived our weeks together almost every night until that feeling of panic became normal, and I stopped trying to remember the dreams."

He gave a heavy sigh, and she hurried on before he could speak.

"I don't expect anything to excuse the fact that we did what we did to you. I don't blame you for wanting revenge, or if you hate me. And now you know everything." She held out her hand. "By order of the MacGregor, I command you to be free of the *djinn* ring. Hand it to me."

Dar cried out in surprise and grabbed his hand. He shook it violently, gingerly bouncing his fingers against the band as if he was being electrocuted. When he finally pulled it off, he tossed it at her. Malina caught it. She felt the hot metal against her palm and dropped it to keep from being burned. The ring fell, but instead of landing on the mattress, it returned to his finger.

"Ok, so the setting you free thing didn't work," Malina said in surprise. She flicked her burned hand a few times. "Do you want me to try to take it off you?" She reached out her hand as if to pull the ring from him.

"No, no, I'm good." He cradled his hand to his chest so she couldn't reach it. "Maybe another time."

"You must hate me now." The pain in her arm wouldn't go away. She massaged the muscle trying to get it to stop.

"I don't hate you," he admitted. "I should, but I don't."

"You'd be justified," she insisted, rubbing her

187

numb arm faster. "I'd hate me if I were you. I mean—"

"Can you stop talking for a moment and let a guy think?" he interrupted.

Malina nodded. "Aye, I can do that." He didn't speak for several seconds, and she couldn't handle the silence. "So what are you thinking about? Because I'd like to point out that you tried to kill me too. Sure, I did it first, but you're doing it second."

He arched a brow. A small smile curled his lips. The expression gave her hope. "The MacGregor reputation is greatly inflated if a couple of ghosts, fairies, and a goblin is considered a legitimate murder attempt."

"You forgot about the bog dweller crawling out of the bathroom floor." Malina naturally leaned into him, wanting a kiss.

He chuckled. "Nice try. I think I'd know if I gave luck to bog dweller. I don't even know what manner of creature that would be."

Malina stopped mid-motion in confusion. "But...?"

"What?"

"I don't get why you're laughing." She distinctly remembered the scary creature pawing

Euann's fuel tank. "There was a bog thing crawling out of the floor of our guest bathroom. I imagine he's made it out of there by now."

His expression fell, and he stood from the bed. "Explain what you mean by bog dweller."

She was slower to stand. "I don't know. His skin looked like lava from a volcano that started to cool when the outside turns black and the cracks glow with red. He was crawling out of some kind of wet portal in the floor. His smell reminded me of the peat bogs. I'm guessing he arrived with the Leprechauns."

Dar took hold of her numb arm to keep her attention on him. "What did this creature say?"

"Say?" She glanced down in distraction. For whatever reason, his touch was easing the tingling sensation.

"Yes, what did he say?" He gave her a little shake as if to demand she focused her attention on what he was asking. His grip tightened.

"Ow!" She jerked her arm away. "Jeez, take it easy. He didn't say anything. He just gurgled at me like he was pissed off and his throat was full of water. It's not like I tried to have a conversation with the thing. I was busy trying to fight off a ghost mob."

"Malina, this is very important." He reached to pull his pants off the floor and slid them over his naked hips. "What other demons have your family tried to kill besides me?"

"None that I know of. We fought a *lidérc* that was trying to use Charlotte and Lydia as vessels to suck the power from Erik and Iain. In recent years, from what I know about, Niall has been hunting leprechauns, a chupacabra, a lizard man of the swamp claiming to be a dragon-shifter from another planet, Bigfoot who turned out to be a hairy human, a vampire, some tree spirit... would the vampire count?"

"No, vampires are vampires, not demons," Dar dismissed. "What else?"

"Jane's mom was a *bean nighe*," she offered, "a banshee."

"Do you think Jane's mom is crawling out of your bathroom floor?" Dar asked a little sarcastically.

"No." Malina grabbed the sweatpants from where they'd landed on the bed and pulled them over her legs.

"What else?"

"I don't know," she said in exasperation. "How far back do you want me to go? I don't remember any other exorcisms beyond yours." She pulled the borrowed t-shirt over her head, feeling frumpy in the baggy clothes. "Do I look like a demon hunter to you?"

"You look like you're about to go for a run," he said, eyeing her attire. "Which is probably a good thing since we need to leave. I feel like our luck is running out here."

Malina rolled the sweats at her waist to make them fit better. She missed her designer shoes and dresses. It was one of the perks of being able to materialize whatever she wanted from a picture—she was always able to look nice. Now, when she stood before the one man whose opinion of her felt the most important, she looked like she'd crawled out of a lost-and-found bin.

"Something feels off." He went to pull back the curtain to peer out the window. "There is a lady in a blue car watching our hotel room."

"Friend of yours?" Malina joined him to see who was there. She frowned. "Dammit. That's Mrs. Callister, the local busybody. She's probably here to see which locals are using the hotel rooms to cheat on their spouses. We can't let her see us."

"What? Ashamed to be seen with your demidemon husband?"

"No. She'll just turn this into something seedy," Malina whispered, wondering if the woman could somehow hear them from across the parking lot. Mrs. Callister undoubtedly had a parabolic microphone strapped to the passenger seat of her car. "Some idiot introduced her to blogging, and she's taken her social reports digital. She's a pest. Her new favorite pastime is writing her weekly Green Vallis gossip column featuring my family. Euann keeps sending her viruses to keep her posts from going viral. The last thing I need is a picture coming out of a hotel room like a call girl."

"Ah, so you're just scared everyone on the Internet will see you in sweatpants coming out of a cheap hotel," he whispered back.

Mrs. Callister lifted a pair of binoculars from her passenger seat and began searching the hotel.

Malina jerked the curtain closed to hide. "Oh, shit. I just thought of something. What if she has been up to the house and saw what happened there? Who knows what's going on with all the protection spells right now."

"I don't think she has," Dar reasoned.

"How can you be so sure?"

"Because if she saw a haunted house, I doubt

she'd be on sleaze patrol at the local hotel." He pulled the curtain aside and pointed. "See, she only seems interested in that one room."

"Huh, I wonder which townsperson is having an affair?" Malina craned her neck to see.

"Probably a good thing she has her column," he teased. "You'll be able to find that out the next time she posts."

"You're being nice to me," Malina observed. "Does this mean you forgive me?"

"It means I recognize that you tried to make a grand gesture by telling me what you did and taking off the *djinn* ring. It would have been nicer if it actually worked, but I'm choosing not to blame that on you."

Suddenly a bright blue light illuminated the surrounding area. A shadow was cast by the hotel building over the parking lot. Mrs. Callister stepped out of her car, her mouth slightly ajar as she gazed into the distance. Several people came out of the hotel. Dar reached the door before Malina could decide whether or not it was a good idea to investigate.

He motioned her to follow. "We can't stay here."

They crossed the parking lot, joining the gathering crowd to look toward the sky. Behind the hotel, miles away, the blue light shone like a spotlight to draw attention.

"What is that?" a woman questioned.

"Aliens?" one man offered in confusion.

"Paranormal mumbo jumbo," Mrs. Callister dismissed.

"I saw something like this in the city once. It's a spotlight that stores use to get people to come to their sale," a woman explained.

"That's not like any spotlight I've ever seen," a man with a cigar put forth. "Come on, Starla, let's go check it out."

Others apparently thought that was a great idea because they disappeared into their rooms only to return with car keys.

"I think that's my house." Malina grabbed Dar's arm and led him toward the cars. "This isn't good. We need to get there first."

"Don't look now, but your friend's got you in her sights." Dar nodded to Mrs. Callister who was blindly reaching into her passenger window as she stared at Malina. She fumbled a moment before pulling out a camera. Dar tried to wave at the busybody, grinning wildly. Malina slapped his hand and pointed across the parking lot behind the woman. Mrs. Callister turned to see what had gotten Malina's attention and Malina used the distraction to jerk Dar around side a parked van to hide before the woman could take a shot. "Where's your car?"

Dar stood to peek inside the van's window before kneeling next to her. He pointed his thumb at the vehicle. "Right here."

Malina glanced at the faded logo on the side. "Harrison's Plumbing, Cooling, and Heating? You're an air conditioner repair man?"

"Didn't you once tell me gambling wasn't a real job?" He grinned.

"I did," she agreed, "but that didn't mean I thought you should add car thief to your résumé."

"Listen, do you want a ride to the house or not? I'm more than happy to walk it. Or we can hitch a ride with Mrs. Callister. I'm sure she'd love to hear all about how we met and—"

"Fine, we take the van," Malina consented, "but remind me to hire Harrison to fix all the plumbing your *gremians* destroy in the house."

Chapter Thirteen

The driveway of the MacGregor home was filled with cars. Dar had to park the stolen van toward the bottom of the drive, and they walked their way up the hill. People had come from all over town to see what was happening. Malina even saw Sheriff Johnson's telltale cowboy hat as he stood near a squad car, scratching his head as if wondering what to do about the gathering. She pulled Dar into the trees to avoid speaking to the man. It wasn't that she didn't like the displaced Southerner, but he tended to ask a lot of questions in a roundabout manner that made conversations last a long time. And they would be questions she didn't have answers to.

The light had not faded and as they approached

the front lawn. The beacon came from the roof, lighting up the night sky, as well as every window. Malina stared up at the house. "It doesn't look like anyone's tried to go inside yet. They must be waiting for a show to start. I suppose I have you to thank for that. Whatever luck you gave me must be holding up. Okay, so what do you need to get started?"

"Started doing what?" Dar frowned.

"Cleaning up your mess." Malina gestured to the home. "Reverse their luck and force the ghosts to leave. Cross them over into the great beyond. Evict their asses. I don't care. Just get them to stop."

Dar gestured helplessly. "Maybe I can? If I can get inside and touch those two little brats who tried to take all my energy while I was sleeping, I might be able to siphon it back. Catching ghosts isn't easy though. I have a feeling they won't want to get too close to me. They sure as hell won't want to get too close to you."

"You're not going in there alone, so don't even bother saying it. Do you think any of them will try to follow us if we go in the front door?" She motioned to where the gathering crowd had stopped to form a semi circle starting at the old oak tree and crossing over the drive to the other side of the lawn. They talked lowly amongst themselves while watching the house like they expected fireworks to go off at any moment.

Unexpectedly, someone jerked her elbow to force her from Dar's side. She gasped in surprise, tensing to fight as she turned. It was Euann.

"I don't think we can hide this," Euann said, unconcerned by her fighting stance. "The entire town is on our lawn."

"Out-of-towners from the hotel too," Malina added. She dropped her fists. "Where's the rest of the family?"

"Cait is watching over Charlotte. Niall is pissed about your new friend, but I think he's circling the gardens out back. Rory is taking a leak in the woods. Raibeart is crazy drunk insisting ya actually got married to a dandy." Euann laughed. "Can ya imagine? Ya? Married? I think we're going to have to commit him to a mental hospital soon."

"Hi." Dar leaned forward and held out his hand. "I'm Darragh Lahey, Malina's husband. You can call me Dar. Nice to meet you."

Malina winced. Euann shook the man's hand

but arched a brow at his sister. Weakly, she exclaimed, "Surprise!"

Euann made a strange noise of disbelief before dismissing, "Aye, nice try. Ya almost had me there for a moment."

"How is Charlotte?" Malina asked before the conversation became any more uncomfortable.

"It's odd, but I think she's better. She seems more... I don't know how to explain it. She's more like the Charlotte we first met."

"That's not saying a lot. If I remember correctly, you guys petrified the poor girl the first night you met her," Malina reminded him. "She woke up thinking she had a horrible nightmare and a monster of a hangover."

"There is that," Euann agreed. "And to be fair, I'm pretty sure that hangover was all her doing. Fun times."

"Not that I don't respect the laid back approach you all are taking to this situation, but isn't anyone worried about the giant blue light coming out of your house?" Dar interrupted. "Or the fact that the locals are starting to inch their way closer to look inside?"

"Oh, it's bad, but we've seen much worse." Euann studied the glowing mansion.

"We've caused worse," Malina said. The sound of the crowd grew louder as their numbers increased. "But he's right. We need to act."

"Too many of them to petrify." Euann glanced around at the crowd. "What about a zombie walk? Do ya think there are enough of us here to mesmerize them all?"

"Probably not." Malina bit her lip thoughtfully. "That's a lot of zombies to control."

"At least it's only ghosts and not a *bean nighe*," Euann said.

"Or a *lidérc*," Malina added. "What about a power surge? We can't very well go with the mass shared hallucination angle again so soon. We'll have the authorities here building a contamination dome over the entire town."

"Northern lights?" Euann said, tilting his head to look at the sky.

"Not with the windows glowing like that," Malina dismissed.

"We could say we were testing a new security system, and it went awry," Rory offered coming from the nearby trees. He slapped Euann on the shoulder. "Anyone who knows ya will believe it."

"I hope ya washed your hands," Euann ducked away from Rory. "Where's Raibeart?"

"He insisted he knew the way here, so my guess is he's up in a tree somewhere five miles south thinking it's his bedroom. The lunatic kept going on and on about how Malina finally managed to snag a man, but it was no surprise that the guy is a foppish dandy lizard or something." Rory gave Malina a sheepish look. "No offense, cousin. Raibeart's words, not mine."

"None taken," she said.

"Well, some taken," Dar mumbled.

"So, we're not killing this one?" Rory nodded at Dar. "Niall didn't seem too happy about that. What about ya, Malina?"

"No. Don't kill him," she said.

"I agree, no killing," Euann inserted. "I kind of like him. He's funny. Dar, tell him what ya told me when I said what Raibeart was going on about."

"That I'm Malina's husband?" Dar asked.

Rory and Euann began laughing, hard.

"See!" Euann slapped Rory hard on the back. "I told ya he's funny."

"What about telling the townspeople the truth?" Dar suggested, drawing their attention to the problem at hand. "It has to be easier than all these elaborate lies."

Rory and Euann laughed harder.

"Can ya imagine?" Euann asked.

"Ladies and gentleman of Green Vallis," Rory announced to their small group with mock pageantry. "We invited ya all here tonight to witness an unearthly laser light show. Behold, the wonders of the afterlife. Proof that ghosts exist and the dead are never really gone. Please don't stampede and trample your neighbors to death as ya panic and run away. Medical professionals are on standby for anyone suffering a mental breakdown from having the safety of your world completely shattered."

"We have to do something." Dar frowned.

"Hey, ya got red on your shirt." Rory pointed to where the blood stained the front of Dar's shirt.

"Yeah, thanks," Dar dismissed. "Nothing you've come up with has been that believable. How about we just call it a natural wonder and go with the less is more approach? Leave it a mystery."

"Feeling guilty that you're the one who caused this?" Niall appeared out of the darkened tree line to join them. "No one is in the gardens yet, which is a good thing because there's a goblin den made out of what looks to be broken pieces of our dining table in the shrubbery. Also, I think he was wearing one of Malina's shirts. Some gold striped number with—"

"No, not my—" Malina began to protest.

"Materialize another one later," Niall interrupted.

Malina's lips tightened in annoyance at her brother's superior look. What did boys know about feeling pretty and being a lady? Men could throw on a kilt, trek through mud, show up at a MacGregor corporate business meeting without showering, and everyone would call him rugged and adventurous. If she pulled her hair back into a ponytail and decided not to bother with makeup, they'd think she was sick and try to send her home.

"All right. Here's what's going to happen," Malina decided. "Rory, you're on crowd control. Find Sheriff Johnson. He was halfway down the drive by his squad car. Mesmerize him and get him to order all his deputies to get these people off our private property and have him put blockades at the end of the drive to keep people from trying to sneak back up. Let them be the ones to spread the story about the power surge in the reserve generators."

"On it," Rory headed down the hill to find the sheriff.

"Euann, you have publicity control," Malina said.

"Ya want me to cause cellphones to glitch?" Euann offered.

"Aye," Malina agreed. "And I'm going to need you to find Mrs. Callister and charm her. I guarantee she is around here somewhere taking pictures. Tell her the house had old wiring and five generators malfunctioned all at once and caused the lights to—make something believable and techy up. Do whatever you have to, but get her onboard before she posts anything online. We don't need our home becoming a paranormal pilgrimage. And see if you can't get her to calm everyone's future fears by saying it's nothing dangerous and the family is going to great lengths to fly in a foremost electrical engineer to look at it. We can make a public apology for any town disturbance later to downplay the issue."

"Why do I have to deal with that gossip mongering busybody?" Euann whined.

"Because Rory wouldn't be able to help himself around Callister. His explanation would involve aliens and sea monsters in an epic battle over humanity. And, before you ask, Niall would probably just stare at her sternly until she was confident he planned on hiding her body in the woods." Malina motioned that he should get moving. "Plus, I think she has a thing for you. Now go."

Euann grumbled but did as she suggested.

"I'll go inside and—" Dar began.

"I don't trust him, Malina," Niall interrupted. "He's the reason this is happening. Order him to stay behind. We don't need his help. This is a family matter."

"He has the power to make them leave," Malina countered. "We need him in there."

"So do I. I can exorcise ghosts. I've done it plenty of times." Niall crossed his arms over his chest. "Tell him to stay out of our way."

"*He* is right here," Dar gritted through clenched teeth. "*He* can hear you."

"Order him to be quiet," Niall warned, turning his full attention on Dar. "I don't want to hear anything he has to say."

"Tell your brother to take his pompous orders and shove them up his—" Dar threatened.

"Both of you shut up!" Malina commanded.

Several people turned to look at them in curiosity. "Help me or get out of my way."

Malina marched along the edge of the crowd toward the front door. A redheaded woman motioned for her attention. "Is it radioactive?"

"Radiation," someone corrected. "Ask her if it's radiation."

"Is it radia—" the redhead began only to stop and *bawk* like a chicken. Her arms lifted and began to flap like wings. "*Bawk, bawk, baa-awk!*"

"What the..." Malina rushed away from the confused woman. Other barnyard sounds came from the crowd.

"Are you making fun of me? Because it sounds like you're making fun of me." The shout was followed by a loud screech. Malina glanced back in time to see the redhead get punched in the face.

"Get off my wife!" a man yelled.

"Hey, she came on to me," another shouted.

The blue glow from the house softened as the crowd, one by one, turned on each other.

"Dammit," Malina swore. "They call this crowd control? I told Rory to mesmerize the sheriff, not convince the crowd to start an all out brawl. Do you see Rory anywhere?"

Dar shook his head in denial. "I don't think it's your family doing this."

"What makes ya say that?" Niall asked.

Dar pointed toward the house. "The fact that you have a chaos demi-demon and a full-blooded discord demon standing in the entryway."

Malina's head whipped around.

"Where did they come from?" Niall demanded. He lifted his shirt and pulled a sharp knife from his waist. The flash of carved steel caused a memory to bounce into Malina's mind. He'd used that knife on Dar to subdue him before setting him on fire. It was a demon blade.

"I believe the chaos demi-demon, Apep, is from Detroit but he likes to pretend he's from a rich neighborhood in Connecticut. He's the one who looks like he's fresh off the runway," Dar answered. "The other one, Andras, in black leather and metal studs is from a place altogether a bit nastier."

"I'm gonna fucking kill you!" a townsman raged. Screams sounded as the fighting intensified tenfold.

"He did this," Niall eyed Dar, his chest lifting in hard breaths as if it took everything he had not to attack. "He brought them here. Raibeart ordered me to leave him unharmed, but I don't care what that old fool says. He can banish me from the clan for disobeying an elder's order in battle, but I'll not let him hurt our family."

Malina loved her brother, but sometimes he could be very old fashioned in his beliefs. However, since that sense of duty would keep him from trying to stab her husband, Malina decided to use it to her advantage.

"If you do anything without infallible proof, I will never forgive you," Malina said.

"Ya call that a threat? Ya said the same thing to Euann when he glamoured away your small toe, and ya thought ya had lost it," Niall taunted. "Sit down little girl and let the men handle things."

"Say something like that to me again and I swear I will smack you into the next century," Malina threatened. Irritation filled her as she remembered all the things Niall had ever done to her over the centuries—from boyish pranks to perceived slights to convincing her to kill her husband. Her full attention shifted to her brother, and the urge to fight became strong.

"Show me what ya got, wee lassie," Niall taunted unconcerned. She desperately wanted to wipe the mocking look of his face. "Like I'd be scared of a warlock that can't even cast a simple love potion magick spell without nearly killing her own brother and his girlfriend. Or how about the time your snake potion exploded and destroyed the wing of our castle?"

"There is nothing wrong with my magick," Malina screamed. "I'm every bit a warlock as you are!"

"Tell that to our missing brother," Niall stated in a harsh voice. "We all know you're the reason Kenneth is gone. Oh, but we can't say anything cause poor little Malina may cry, and we can't have that."

Malina gasped, her hands balling into fists. She felt as if she'd been struck in the gut. "How dare you blame me for Kenneth. I tried to help him. I tried!"

"A fat lot of good your help did," Niall quipped. "Do me a favor, if I'm in trouble, don't try to assist."

"Oh, don't worry. You're in trouble right now, and I can guarantee you I'm not going to stop beating you until you take back every rotten thing you've ever said to me!" Malina leaped forward, hands raised to strike.

Chapter Fourteen

"Stop it," Dar shouted to interrupt the growing argument between brother and sister. He shot forward to pull Malina back before she did something she'd regret. "Neither of you mean what you are saying. I should have seen this earlier, but their nearness doesn't affect me. That discord you're feeling right now is misdirected. These feelings are what transpire when non-demon-bloods are in Andras's presence. What do you think is happening behind us? Everyone here will work themselves into a frenzy, and they won't recall even seeing Andras let alone that he influence them to do it. I know it's hard, but try to keep a level head."

"Stay out of this," Malina ordered. "This is

between my brother and me, and it's well overdue."

"*Thalla 's cagainn bruis,*" Niall added. "Ya heard her. Get lost. This is none of your concern. It's MacGregor business."

Dar was more worried about the two demons on the doorstep than he was about Niall the Neanderthal's mounting anger. When Malina described the bog-man coming from the floor, he'd been concerned that it might have been a creature clawing its way from the fire realm. He had hoped his luck would hold out and that it really was a bog dweller.

"Stupid ghost brats," he muttered. Dar needed an infusion of good luck, but this chaotic crowd was not the place to try to get some. He looked at Niall. Brother and sister were yelling at each other in Gaelic, reciting grievances that had to have occurred nearly three hundred years prior. Dar took a cautious step around the siblings before reaching out to touch Niall's back. The man jerked, but Dar managed to pull good luck from the angry warlock. As Niall turned, Malina landed a punch on his jaw.

Dar couldn't help but grin. "Sorry, champ, but

your sister is going to win this fight. Maybe next time you'll think twice before trying to kill me."

Malina punched a second time before Niall could form an answer.

He knew the moment Apep's and Andras's eyes found him. A cold chill worked its way up his spine. Common sense told him to run away, and to take Malina with him. It was also the cowardly thing to do.

"Stay here, Malina," Dar commanded, wishing it sounded less like an order the second the words left his mouth. For once he hoped she'd listen to him.

"Bite me, Dar," Malina retorted. She took a step toward the house. "I'm not scared of a little chaos and discord."

"Still trying to prove yourself worthy of being a MacGregor?" Dar taunted, trying anything to make her come to her senses. "Just going to march impulsively into danger so that Niall will have to come and rescue you again."

"What is he talking about?" Niall rubbed his jaw.

"Nothing. Dar is being an ass." Malina glared at Dar, only to start bickering with her brother again. "And no, Niall, that doesn't mean I want you to kill him for me now."

"I didn't ask if I could kill him, but now that ya mention it—" Niall defended.

"Everything is death and killing with you," Malina interrupted. "Complain, complain, stomp around, complain, and demand to always have your way. There are no shades of gray in your black and white views. Everyone is either good or evil, with you or against you, a screw-up or—"

"Oh, I'd say ya are very much a screw-up," Niall put forth with a snort, "and I'm always cleaning up your relationship messes."

"I never asked you to," she cried. "You never give me a chance to take care of myself. That's your whole overbearing mode of operation, Niall. All of you take great pleasure in trying to tell me how wrong I am. Since I was born with a birthmark on my ass, witch hunters came after me. That meant it was my fault Aunt Elspeth died getting me to England. I was raised British, so it's my fault I'm not Scot enough to be a real MacGregor. I can't possibly understand the clan ways."

"*Is cuma liom sa diabhal,*" Niall muttered. "I don't care if your feelings are hurt. We treat ya like a child because ya act like a child. If ya want to be seen as an adult then grow up. Ya make bad decisions Malina, and ya always have. Ya are reckless and wild, with no thought of how your actions affect the rest of us. Case and point, ya married a fucking demon."

"Well, I have news for you, you're never going to be able to kill Dar because I love him," she declared. "I love him! And you're just going to have to learn to live with that fact. I love a demon."

"Dar, don't stand out there with all the mortals. Do come say hello," Andras called. "It's been a long time."

Malina's declaration gave him immense pleasure, but he wished she'd stop yelling it. He didn't want her bringing demonic attention to herself. Malina and Niall might fight but had to believe they wouldn't kill each other. She was safer outside having her moment of sibling rivalry than in the house. Dar straightened his suit and lifted his chin as he went to where he was summoned.

"I see you received our invitation." Andras grinned. The demon snapped his fingers, and the blue beacon disappeared, leaving the lawn in darkness compared to what it had been before.

Should Andras change out of his leather vest

and pants, he would be the complete picture of normality. Though tall and broad, his human disguise was deceptively unmemorable. Strands of hair were combed over to hide his balding head. He was neither ugly nor handsome, neither fat nor thin. If a person had no reason to talk to him, they would probably not recall what he looked like. However, right now, he resembled a middle-aged man on his way to a bondage convention.

"What brings you guys to town?" Dar asked as if he didn't already know.

Apep's unconcerned posture was deceiving. "Like you could keep a place this powerful all to yourself. I'm surprised at you, Darragh. You used to be so cool."

"I love it when you boys argue," Andras said, stepping back and lifting his hand to invite Dar into the home as if he was the new owner.

"Would it help if I apologized?" Dar asked.

"It might." Apep gave a little pout.

"Then I'm sorry," Dar said. "That wasn't cool of me."

"Thank you," Apep accepted the apology.

"Come inside out of the mosh pit," Andras insisted. "We'll let the humans play for a while. It is a beautiful thing, but they do tend to get loud."

Inside the house was a ruin of what it had once been. The marble floors were cracked as if the earth had torn apart beneath the foundation. What few light fixtures that had not been ripped from the walls flickered with intermittent power. A fire pit burned in the middle of the front hall, giving light and heat to the large space. The banister had fallen off both sides of the stairs and lay in pieces on the floor.

"Beautiful, isn't it?" Andras asked though it wasn't a question. "I had to relocate a goblin to the back gardens and exorcise some ghosts, but other than that it was what they call move-in ready. I hear I have you to thank for that. Genius really, giving luck to ghosts and lower level supernaturals like you did. You must have been building up your power stores for years."

"Decades," Dar corrected, thinking of how he'd spent all those years in Vegas hoarding extra luck so he could come get his revenge. It looked like he was going to receive that long-standing wish. The irony was, he no longer wanted revenge. If he were honest, he never truly wanted to retaliate. He'd told himself he did so that he felt warranted in coming after her. Despite every-thing, he had never stopped loving her. All he wanted in this world was the chance to be with Malina.

"Impressive," Andras allowed. "I have been trying to break into this location for years and thanks to you and your luck, here I am. Had I known you had so much ambition to prove yourself a real demon, I would have paid more attention to you. Seducing a MacGregor warlock for information, patiently siphoning enough luck so no one would notice you were doing it, and then sneaking here to crack open a portal so that demons may have access to the ley lines? You are a true dark artist."

Dar had been trying to do none of those things. Nonetheless, in the presence of one so formidable, a demon who even now stirred the darker longings inside Dar's most primal of powers, he felt it best not to point that fact out. So far, neither demon was trying to kill him, and he'd like to keep it that way.

"Daddy's here. Have great fear," singsong voices chanted from above and the sound of small feet bounced across the landing. Dar frowned. He'd thought Andras had evicted all the spirits. The ghost children couldn't be seen, only heard.

"He will rip you ear to ear. Limb to limb. End to end."

"Quiet girls," Andras ordered with a small smile of parental approval. "Daddy's working."

The ghost girls giggled.

Daddy? Dar thought. *Figures.*

"My daughters are very impressed by you, and they do not impress easily," Andras admitted. "I've had them here keeping an eye on things for me."

"So was that you they saw crawling out of the bathroom floor?" Dar asked conversationally. "I wasn't expecting that."

"No, that was me," Apep said a little bitterly. "And I can say I didn't expect to have to be clawing my way back from hell because someone I thought was my friend decided to send me packing."

"I took a more direct route," Andras gestured toward the crevice in the floor. "I don't care for the bog lands separating the realms. The moisture and heat aren't good on my leathers."

"Daddy, please, don't make us stay." One of the girls appeared, looking as innocent and precious as any human child.

"We so do wish to go and play," the second one joined in, also emerging from nothingness.

"Fine, but no killing," Andras instructed. "Daddy needs the disharmony to get big and strong."

The girls giggled and ran out the front door without bothering to open it.

"Do you have children?" Andras asked. When both men shook their heads in denial, he added, "They are so much work."

Dar highly doubted the demon of discord was an attentive father, especially knowing his children had been running around Earth tormenting humans and playing on the ley lines while daddy was in the fire realm.

"What are the little hellions' names?" Apep asked.

Andras appeared confused for a moment and frowned. "One is E-vil-ah-something. I think the other girl is named... Jeffery? It'll come to me. Who can remember these things?"

Dar managed to glance at the door without drawing too much notice to his concern for Malina. He hoped her brother was taking it easy on her. She talked tough, but she always reminded him of a delicate little flower. Or course, he'd never tell her that.

"Now, what do you say we find something to drink," Andras offered. "I'm sure the former tenants must have left something behind."

Andras strode ahead of them, revealing the fact that oval holes had been cut out of the backside of his black leather pants. There was nothing to obstruct the view of his two tanned cheeks. One had the tattooed face of an owl on it and the other a pair of angel wings. Dar coughed, trying to hide his surprise.

Apep gave him a cynical look of understanding. Under his breath, he said, "Don't ask him about it. They're into some pretty weird shit in the fire realm, and some stories can't be unheard."

Chapter Fifteen

Malina screamed at the top of her lungs as she pinned Niall to the ground by pressing her knees on his stomach. She then proceeded to strike his shoulders and chest with her fists. He didn't fight back as he moaned in a daze. "How dare you take away the one thing in this stupid life that I've ever loved, and who ever loved me? You and your bull-shit missions and sense of honor." As she struck, magick lit up around her hands to compound the impact. "You told me he was evil. You promised me you had proof. You made me believe..." She sniffed back tears as her strikes became weaker. "You made me give him up." She sniffed again. "You forced me to choose between my heart and my family, and it was all for nothing. He's not who you said he was, whom you *swore* to me on our family honor that he was. He didn't kill anyone and how is he ever going to trust me? I led him to his death." She took a sharp, shaky breath as her animosity toward Niall turned inward. "How's he ever going to love me again? I don't deserve it. Euann's right. I'm never going to have love. I remember all of it now. I brought him to you and didn't stop you from stabbing him. We set him on fire and the smell..."

She swayed weakly as the memory completely flooded her senses. The front lawn turned into desert sand, and the dark sky turned to dusk. The red fire in the desert grave roared angrily as she looked down into it. Dar was dead. She wanted to jump in and die too.

"I feel dizzy," she whispered.

Malina fell to the side. She wasn't sure how long she lay in darkness, but when she came to she was again on the MacGregor lawn. Dar was alive. Fate had given her another chance.

People still argued around them, some becoming more violent, some crying and screeching. They were lost in their heightened states.

However, Malina's anger had all turned inward where it belonged. Somehow that feeling of self-hate broke whatever enchantment the discord demon had wrought over her.

"Niall?" She crawled to her brother to touch his face. He blinked heavily before again closing his eyes. She remembered slamming him pretty hard with concentrated balls of magick. There had been a lot of pent-up feelings behind the attack, and she doubted he'd wake up anytime soon.

"Dar?" Malina glanced at the house, half expecting him to be where she'd last seen him—walking toward the front door. The blue glow was gone from the house, and instead, the gentle flicker of orange firelight had replaced it inside the windows.

Malina didn't think as she grabbed the demon blade from her brother's waist and ran toward the house. She placed her ear to the door and listened. A fairy tried to buzz past her face to distract her. Its red eyes shone in the dark. Malina squished it against the door to stop its racket before wiping her hand on her sweatpants.

Although she couldn't hear voices, she felt

Dar as surely as if she stood next to him. Malina pushed through the door and followed her feelings toward the dining room. She chanced a small peek around the corner before quickly hiding. The three demons sat on chairs with no table. Broken bits of wood and car parts were thrown haphazardly around the room.

"No, I swear it," Apep affirmed. "The saying at the time was, *luck be a Leahy* because he helped some high rollers hit big in order to score us some sweet concert tickets. Someone misunderstood and started saying *luck be a lady*. I had no idea you had bigger plans back them. I thought you were just a happy-go-lucky party boy. Had I known, I would have offered to help."

Malina tried to peek a second time, wanting to make sure Dar was unharmed.

"What is she doing in here?" Andras demanded as his eyes narrowed in on Malina. He stood from his chair. "Why isn't she discontent?"

"Your powers mean nothing to me," she announced with mock bravado. In reality, she was terrified. The two demons standing next to her husband looked as if they wanted to rip her apart with their bare hands. By sheer willpower, she stayed upright. Part of her wished that her family would come charging in like they normally did to rescue her. For all she wanted to be seen as a powerful warlock, she was terrified.

"Get rid of her," Andras ordered.

Apep tried to obey.

Dar charged, slamming into the chaos demon. "Don't touch her!"

Apep fought back. Malina rushed forward, wielding the blade. Dar reached out his hand, and she tossed it to him. He cut Apep on the shoulder. The demon howled as his face morphed into the hideous shape of his true form. Dar threw Apep from the dining room.

Andras's form shifted into a fierce winged beast with a head that roughly resembled a wrinkled, featherless owl. He attacked Dar for daring to disobey him.

"Dar, by order of the MacGregor, I command you not to die," Malina yelled. Magick came from the ring in the form of red smoke to force him to obey. Andras's talon made contact, slashing through Dar's chest. It should have been a deadly blow, but the wound instantly healed. Andras growled and slashed again.

Dar cried out in pain but did not sustain injuries. Horns thrust out of his head as he too changed forms.

She gasped as long teeth protruded from his extended mouth. The image of this manifestation triggered the last of her locked memories. She'd seen his demon, and it had alarmed her to know something so fierce could be living inside her husband. She'd let that fear panic her decisions in those final moments.

Malina would not make that mistake again. She didn't have time to fear the change in him. She dove forward and touched his arm. Andras tried to swing at her, but Dar blocked the blow.

"All the luck I have is yours," Malina said, giving him her everything. "And I'm the luckiest woman alive because I've had the pleasure of loving a man like you."

Dar growled as he thrust the blade forward. The lucky aim struck Andras in the chest, and he let out a mighty roar as he began to shake. The demon's molten blood melted the metal, and the handle fell on the ground with a clank.

Dar swept Malina into an arm covered with hard brown skin and propelled her from the dining room. Apep lay on the floor next to the broken staircase. Seeing Dar in his demon form, he grunted and held up his hands. "Not cool, dude."

Dar's body shifted forms, and he returned to his human self. He panted for breath. "That shifting thing never gets easier."

"What about him?" Malina nodded toward Apep.

"What about me?" Apep demanded. He held his bleeding shoulder and stood up. "I'll tell you what about me. I'm taking my sexy ass to the airport and getting on the first flight out of here before one you decides to cut it off." He continued to complain as he stormed out of the front of the house. "So not cool, man. Not cool!"

"The sheriff is here. He's arresting some people for disorderly conduct and making others go home," Niall said. "I found Rory and Euann. They're a little rough for wear but alive. I have them overseeing the evacuation."

"Daddy?" two voices yelled in unison. "Daddy?"

The twin spirits whisked through the house toward the dining room. Niall instantly went to give chase. Malina and Dar were right behind him.

The girls hovered above the bubbling puddle of demon blood near the hilt of the demon dagger.

"Daddy dear, have no fear, we will bring you back to here—*ahh!*"

A force reached forth from the blood and grabbed hold of the little hellions. It jerked them hard into the bubbling puddle and their screams instantly silenced.

"Good riddance." Malina sighed in relief.

"Oh, man, I liked that knife," Niall said, rushing over to pick up the hilt of his destroyed weapon.

"I'll buy you a new demon blade," Malina said.

"Or not," Dar suggested quietly, not letting go of her as he kept his arm around her shoulders. "No reason to arm my brother-in-law who hates me."

"He doesn't hate you," Malina said. "Well, ok, he might, but he will come around."

"Do ya know how hard it is to find demon steel?" Niall asked.

"Be happy it went to save the family." Malina looked around the destroyed home. "Ma and da are going to be so pissed when they get back. That's what you should be worried about. Not an old weapon."

Niall dropped the broken hilt and turned his

full attention to Dar. "It looks like we owe ya a bit of gratitude for helping rid the house of..." Niall motioned to the blood on the floor.

"You're welcome—" Dar started to accept when Niall cut him off.

"But since you're the one who caused all this, I guess that kind of makes the whole gratitude thing null and void." Niall gave a small nod of approval. "I still don't like my sister married to a demon, so I'll be keeping an eye on ya, but as far as demons go, I guess you're not as bad as some."

"Uh, thanks?" Dar answered.

"Don't get comfortable. I may not be intending to kill ya now, but if ya hurt her..." Niall let his word trail off meaningfully.

"Fair enough," Dar said. The men locked eyes for several moments before they each nodded as if they came to an unspoken alpha male understanding.

"Do you think they re-rented our hotel room?" Malina led him toward the door. "There is no way I'm staying here tonight. Plus, we need to return the van to Harrison. I have a feeling we might need him after looking at this place. It's going to take a lot of magick and time to whip this house back into shape."

"I'm betting luck will be on our side." Dar grinned.

"Damn," Rory appeared through the door. "Look at this place."

"I'm not sleeping here tonight," Euann announced, joining Rory briefly in the entryway. "If ya need me, I'll be crashing at Erik and Lydia's. I feel dirty. Mrs. Callister kept trying to touch me, and I need to forget tonight ever happened."

The sound of Euann's footsteps quickly dissipated.

"Are ya going to remind him about the *gremians?*" Malina asked Rory.

Her cousin grinned and headed toward the stairs. "Nah, I think he'll remember it soon enough."

"Can I confess one last thing?" she asked as Dar led her out the door to the nearly empty lawn.

"Do I want to know?" Dar forced a worried frown.

"You are ass ugly in demon form," she said with a laugh.

"I'll have you know, doll face, I'm considered damn hot among demons." Dar grinned, pulling her closer.

"Well, I much prefer you like this," she whispered, leaning up to kiss him.

"Looking like a human?" he supplied.

"No, as my husband standing next to me." Malina gazed deeply into his eyes. "I love you, Dar. Since that first confession, I have loved you."

Chapter Sixteen

EPILOGUE

Dar rushed into the room he shared with his wife in MacGregor mansion and slammed the door. They were in the middle of repairs, but it was slow going. Much of the plant life was dormant for the winter, and they didn't want to kill off the entire forest trying to fix the ruined mansion. Though the room was clean, it had rips in the wallpaper and splintered molding. A mystery stain on the wall looked like someone had splatted a ball of black tar. There was not much she could do for the time being. The common rooms were being renovated first, with those seen by any visiting outsiders receiving priority.

Malina glanced up from where she lay on the bed and chuckled. Dar had his ear pressed to the wood and was breathing hard. Her mother had insisted he don the MacGregor tartan while representing the local charity she was trying to establish. The kilt he wore had smears of white paint as if he'd run into a wall during whatever great escape he was now at the tail end of.

"That kilt looks good on you," Malina said, leaning over to get a better view of his legs. Damn, but her husband was sexy. A thousand years wouldn't cool her ardor for him. "Do me a favor and give it a little shake."

When he turned, his eyes were rounded in fear. "Quick, cast a protection spell so this door can't be opened."

Malina did no such thing as she turned back to her magazine to nonchalantly flip a page. "I warned you that no good deed goes unpunished, but you wanted to be the noble son-in-law."

"What was I supposed to say? She blames me for the house being wrecked, and for the entire town being suspicious of this family, and for the paranormal investigators Euann keeps having to chase off the property." Dar gestured around the room. "I have to make it right somehow. They're your family, and you're my wife. And, when you refused to let her throw us a second wedding, I had to do something to smooth things over. She wanted to start a local charity to help with family PR and to give back to the community, well, so be it. Now that I think about it, she probably blames me for the wedding thing too. She keeps making comments about doves and garland and how pretty it would be to host events in the back garden someday."

"No, trust me. My saying no to her stupid second wedding idea is all on me," Malina assured him.

"Don't you want to marry me again?" he asked.

"Let's not chance it. The last wedding night didn't go too well. Besides, things have worked out as they are meant to be. We have each other. You are my handsome, sexy husband—"

"And you are my brilliant, lovely, aggravating wife," he inserted. "But if it makes her happy to do a small ceremony for us..."

"I love her. She's my ma. I do not want to be lifted up on a fluffy white cloud in angel wings while a choir of cherubs sings medieval ballads for forty minutes and shoots a bridge of arrows for me to float slowly under. At which time the flame of eternal love would be passed around, and everyone would give a prepared speech on the beauty of marriage. Gold glitter would rain down on us as we say our vows, bags of which will be dropped by spellbound doves."

He arched a brow.

"I'm not kidding. I saw the wedding planner book she kept for me once. That was idea number sixty-three, and trust me when I say it was the best one. If you think the angel wings are bad, I'm pretty sure she had the groom in a silk diaper thing and furs to mimic the cherub theme."

Dar looked stricken. "Would she settle for a compromise? We could have a simple ceremony."

Malina laughed by way of response. Margareta did nothing halfway or simple. "I told you before you even met her that she would try to manipulate you with guilt into doing something you'd later regret. That's all she's doing, and it's working. You'll have to learn to say no."

"I thought you were exaggerating about her, but you weren't. This isn't just a guilt trip. I think your ma might actually want me dead." He looked more concerned than the numerous times Niall had threatened his life. "What is with everyone in your family trying to kill me all the time? Did I tell you Lydia blames me for the *gremians* wrecking her lotion supply?"

"That is your fault," Malina pointed out. "As is the goblin who won't leave the back gardens."

"How much luck does everyone think I have? Your ma has me infusing so many people that —*shh!*" He pressed his ear to the door to listen. Whispering, he said, "I think she's coming for me. Tell her I'm not here."

"I take it today's charity work did not go like you thought it would." Malina didn't lower her voice. The footsteps belonged to Rory, not her ma, so she wasn't too concerned. If anything, Malina knew how to avoid her mother.

"After we establish Wisconsin, she wants me to fly to the family charities in Africa with her, then Singapore, then a jaunt through Eastern Europe. I don't know how to tell her that I'm almost tapped out just handling the central Wisconsin area. There is only so much good luck to go around, and she has me siphoning in all the bad. I tell you, doll face, she's cunning. She must be trying to kill me with my own powers because I married you without her blessing. I didn't understand fully when you said you were the only daughter and that made you a delicate flower to be protected."

Malina, seeing his concern wasn't going to ebb, sat up and faced him. "Tell me why you think my ma is trying to kill you."

"All the bad luck I have to take in. Today a chandelier almost fell on my head when Erik and Iain became distracted while installing it, something exploded in the kitchen, something exploded in the bathroom, a pipe burst in the living room—*yes, the living room*—and the front door blew open with a gust of wind and knocked me on the head." He lifted his hair to show her the red mark. "The only competent worker down there is Harrison, and we're trying to hide all hints of magick from him, so that means I have to absorb every unlucky thing he might run into as well. Any more bad luck and I'm not going to live to see our sixtieth wedding anniversary coming up."

"I think you mean fifty-eight," Malina put forth. She reached to her side and flipped a couple of more pages.

"What are you doing in here, anyway?" He paused to listen one last time before lightly tiptoeing to the bed.

"I want new clothes," Malina said, grabbing

the magazine. "The ghost destroyed my wardrobe. Everything is either ripped, stained, or dripping with ectoplasm, and I'm trying to replace the pieces I lost."

Dar eyed the large stack of outfits and accessories she'd already materialized. "How many business suits do you need?" He lifted a pair of pants that would be too short for her. "Is there something you should tell me? Are you shrinking?"

"I'm making some of it for a shelter that helps women find jobs and dress for the interviews. I normally do it, but this shipment will keep my parents from getting mad about my using magick for selfish reasons. Don't worry," she said. Malina lifted her hand to touch a cute retro dress with cherries on the white material. "Ooh, now this is pretty."

"Wait a minute." He frowned as he picked up a suit jacket from the pile. "This doesn't look like anything a woman would wear."

"Surprise?" she said, trying not to look guilty.

"I have clothes," he stated.

"Well, yeah, I was going to talk to you about that. Now, baby, you know I love you, but it's time for you to join the new century. Your suits are..."

she tried to think of a delicate way to phrase her thoughts.

"I like my suits," he protested. "They're hand tailored by the best there ever was in Vegas. You can't find them like this anymore."

"Raibeart is right. You look like a lounge lizard," Malina blurted. "And they are starting to get holes in them. This last week was not kind to anyone's wardrobe."

"But...?" He crossed to a chair where his favorite jacket hung and brushed it off with the back of his hand. "I thought maybe you could use a little magick to fix that."

"Dar, are ya in there?" Margareta yelled. A knock sounded on their door.

Dar shook his head in denial, begging Malina with his eyes to be quiet.

Malina frowned and slid off the bed. She opened the door to face her mother. "Hi, ma. Every time I see you, you look better and better. Those regeneration treatments did the trick."

On the surface, Margareta MacGregor's petite form hardly looked intimidating enough to cause grown men to quake in their boots, but she had a way about her that made people want to obey. A worker passed behind her in the hall humming a tune.

Margareta waited until the man had passed before speaking. "I need Dar. There are some people I want him to meet downstairs in the—"

"About that. Dar thinks you are trying to kill him because you're forcing him to take on so much bad luck," Malina stated bluntly. Her mother looked as if she would argue, so she rushed on, "He doesn't want to disappoint you, so he'd do it if it was up to him, but I'm not going to let him."

"Let me talk to him," she said.

"Sorry. If I learned anything from watching you with my father, it's how to get my way in a marriage. He's done for now."

Her mother gave her a look that was a cross between annoyance and pride.

"If you ever, *ever*, want any chance of me giving you grandchildren over the next say twenty to fifty years, then I'm going to need my husband alive and well."

"Grandchildren?" Margareta repeated, her face lighting up.

"Yeah, Dar wants a bunch of them. I'm not so sure, but he's—" Malina could barely get the words out.

"Do ya know what ya two need? A nice trip away from all this construction. Think of it as an overdue honeymoon. I'll make the arrangements. Ya just relax and be ready to go in a couple of days." Margareta started to leave only to pause. "Ya know, there is something about that lad that I like. I can't quite place it, but..." She gave an approving nod.

"Sounds great, ma, thank you." Malina tried to shut the door, but Margareta stopped her.

"So, does Dar need help finding a ring for ya?" her ma inquired, not for the first time. "A wife really should wear a ring. It's what's done."

"That's enough, ma." Malina shut the door and waited a few seconds until they had privacy. She smiled and gave a playful blink of her lashes as she turned to look at him. "I did mention I love you, right?"

"Once or twice." He grinned. "Thank you for that."

"If you want to thank me, how about you help me pick out some of these clothes?" She crossed over to one of the tabbed magazines.

"Why won't you let me pick out a ring for you instead?" he asked.

"I wanted to pass an idea by you. Since you

have a ring that doesn't come off, figured it would only be fair if I did the same." She gave a small laugh. "We go to the tattoo parlor next week for my appointment."

"The fact that it will annoy your ma has nothing to do with it, I suppose?"

"Ah, well, that is a bonus," she admitted. "But I want everyone to know that I'm yours forever." She held up a picture of a woman modeling skimpy underwear. "Now, back to your clothing choices. What do you think about this?"

He chuckled and mimicked the model's sexy pose. "I suppose I can try one or two new looks."

"Perfect!" Malina laughed. She crossed to a pile she'd made near the corner of the bed and pulled out a stack of male clothing she'd been hiding from him. "I was hoping you'd say that." She began picking through it. "Now, put this on with this one, and, oh, try the kilt with this jacket. You will look so handsome in this color, I think, and—"

"Can we do this later? Now that I'm off the hook for work, an old friend of ours from back in the Vegas days has a telethon coming on soon, and I want to watch. He's big in France." He grinned, and she knew he was teasing her.

"A telethon? Did you honestly just say you would rather watch television than play dress up with your wife?" Malina pouted.

Dar grabbed her from across the pile of clothes she carried in her arms and pulled her face to his. He kissed her passionately until she tossed the clothes to the side and moved in closer. The feel of his body to hers was perfection.

This was home. This was forever. This was love.

"You win. You can try them on later," she said when the kiss broke. "For now, let's just get you out of this dirty kilt."

"As my wife wishes," Dar answered. "Forever as you wish."

The End

Warlocks MacGregor® Series

WARLOCKS MACGREGOR® 5: SPIRITS AND SPELLS

Charlotte Carver is going insane—suffering with everything from memory loss, to hallucinations, to phantom conversations she can't recall having. Something tells her it's not a coincidence that it all started when the MacGregor family moved to town, and the one person who knows what's going on is the last person Charlotte would ask for help. Her new landlord, Niall MacGregor, is not the most approachable man but that hasn't stopped the brooding Scottish biker from invading her dreams.

Motorcycle riding werewolf, Niall MacGregor is the longtime supernatural enforcer for his warlock family. He has regretted more than a few things he's done in the name of duty, but taking Charlotte's memories is the biggest. It was necessary, to both protect the family and save Charlotte's sanity. But the intimate glimpse into her mind has only made him want things he can never have—including the gorgeous, brave woman herself.

When luck finds Charlotte's memories returning, her attraction to Niall explodes, thrusting her into a magickal world. There is little time to adjust as another of Niall's past regrets has come back to threaten everything they hold dear.

Warning: Contains yummy, hot, mischievous MacGregors who are almost certainly up to no good on their quest to find true love.

For more information, visit www.
MichellePillow.com

Warlocks MacGregor® 5: Spirits and Spells Extended Excerpt

Green Vallis, Wisconsin

"*They're a cult.*"

The distorted words hung in the musty air like sagging cobwebs, but Charlotte Carver heard them as clearly as she felt the damp air on her skin. They sounded like they came from an old record player that had seen better days. And to make things even spookier, they were whispered in *her* voice.

Her memory had been shoddy as of late, to say the least, but she was sure that she would remember having a conversation about cults. She looked around and was able to discern from the stone foundation that she was in a basement. The dusky light seemed to drain color from her surroundings.

Charlotte felt the texture of a rope against her hand and glanced down. Her fingers were empty. She felt heavy, like her legs were made of lead. The notion that she wouldn't be able to move very far if she tried haunted her, almost to paralysis.

"They're going to sacrifice us," her raspy voice continued against pops and scratches of the record. Water dripping into a puddle somewhere only added to the eerie ambiance. *"We have to get out of here."*

"I don't understand," Charlotte said. None of this made sense.

"We don't know that." Lydia Barratt was her best friend. She knew that voice better than her

own, even as the recording warped it. No, it was Lydia MacGregor now.

"Lydia?" Charlotte called. "Are you there? What is this place? What are we hearing?"

"I heard them. When they brought me here, they told me my sacrifice would be appreciated. They're sick." Again, Charlotte knew her own voice, but had no memory of the conversation.

"Hello, anyone? What is this place?" she yelled at the top of her lungs. "What is happening?"

"Ya don't need to be here," a man responded, much calmer than her voice had been.

She recognized the Scottish accent of Niall MacGregor, her landlord, and the brother of Lydia's new husband. His words were stronger, clearer than the recording. What was he doing here, in this basement from a black and white horror movie with her?

Niall made her nervous. Hell, he could make anyone nervous. He had a commanding presence that filled a room, even when he didn't say a word.

Sometimes, when he looked at her, she felt as if she would be less exposed if she were standing naked in front of a hundred people. Not that Niall had ever seen her naked. That was just how confident his knowing gaze was.

Charlotte searched her surroundings, looking for him. The room was empty.

Light streaming through a small window revealed an old furnace and water heater in the corner. Next to it were some wooden stairs leading out of the basement. Charlotte tried to go toward them. "Lydia, are you down here? I see a way out."

Suddenly, iron bars fell from the ceiling, blocking off the exit. Charlotte covered her ears as the clanging of metal on the stone floor rang around the small basement. The impact shook the ground and reverberated up through the floor and her legs, shaking every part of her. She looked up and down in a panic. The bars only fortified her fear that she was being held captive in the torture chamber of a house of horrors.

"This door does not exist within ya anymore," Niall said. His green eyes appeared first out of the shadows, bright in color but lacking the teasing light common to the other men in his family. His brown hair fell to his chin, and she had the impression that it was more out of neglect than a style choice. His kilt looked well worn. For a man from a wealthy family, he seemed to go out of his way to look like he didn't come from money. Still, on the surface, he was handsome, rugged, and moody. Whenever he came to Green Vallis, he drew attention like a movie star bad boy, riding into town on his motorcycle, returning from some mysterious adventure.

None of these things impressed Charlotte, for they were surface dressing. All the MacGregor men were handsome. If she was interested in a pretty face, there were several single ones to choose from—Euann and Rory were both sweet and amiable, dressed in designer clothing, and appeared to like having a good time. And they smiled at her. Niall never smiled.

Like now. He was definitely not smiling as he looked at her. "Ya do not want to go beyond this room."

"But..." She pointed at the door, only to see it disappear. Water dripped again, a solitary ambiance that caused the dread inside of her to intensify.

"And ya do not need these bars, or these windows," he said. "Ya do not need this night. Let it go, Charlotte."

"Where's Lydia?" She looked around. Panic

filled her. None of this was as it should be. "I heard her. Where is she? I have to find her."

Charlotte ran to the window and grabbed hold of the sill. Her fingers felt the strain as she pulled herself up before bracing her toes in the stone foundation to hold a precarious position. Outside, she saw Lydia's lawn.

That's weird.

Lydia owned an old Victorian house, and her basement looked nothing like the one Charlotte was currently inside.

A blue light flashed past where she looked and she gasped, almost slipping. She held on tighter. Lightning flashed across the landscape, blowing tree limbs over like toothpicks across the grass, as a windstorm raged.

"Ya cannot keep coming back here, Charlotte," Niall said from behind her. "Leave it buried. Stop digging."

A demonic creature's face appeared in the window. Charlotte cried out as she lost her grip. She fell back, unable to look away. It was half man, half panther, and one hundred percent terrifying. His eyes glowed like embers and his sharp fangs glistened in the dark as, behind him, lightning struck closer than before. A clawed hand pressed to the glass, lighting it up with an ominous, foreboding glow.

"Let us out!" her recorded voice yelled, but no sound would come from her trembling lips.

"I told ya to stop looking." Niall appeared before her, blocking the creature in the window. He reached out as if to touch her. "I would take it all back if I could. I would rewind time. I—"

Charlotte gasped and flung her arms as she came out of a deep sleep, trying to swat the invisible hand that pulled away from her cheek. It took a moment to realize she fought a dream that wasn't there. The smell of a basement stayed with her as she turned on the mattress. Eventually, her breathing evened itself out.

Her empty bedroom held very little; one could say it had a minimalist's touch—a lavender-scented candle left burning too long, a crumpled paperback discarded when she fell asleep, and a butcher knife on her nightstand. She vaguely remembered putting the knife there, but it wasn't the first time her tired mind had felt the need to protect itself by rejecting reality.

The silence of downtown streets below resonated with a shiver that ran up her spine. For a moment, she second-guessed the glow of the streetlights that fell across her bed, imagining the shadow of a spidery creature. The hour was late and here she was again in the arms of insomnia. Sadly, she hadn't slept a full night in a long time. In fear, she gazed wearily at the window as if expecting there to be something or someone outside the glass, standing two stories tall looking in on her, waiting for the right time to reach inside.

The whisper of the voice still lingered, but the images leading up to it faded before she could hold on to them. *"I would take it all back if I could. I would rewind time."*

"Take it all back," she whispered, unable to recall what the words might have referred to.

There are aches that cannot be described, pains that settle in the stomach and chest caused by nothing more than a faded memory. Charlotte knew there was something she should recall, like a scary movie she watched through her fingers as a child—but its plot she could no longer recall. She remembered the feeling though, the unfounded fear. It crept in every time she closed her eyes.

There was something she needed to remember.

Why couldn't she remember?

Charlotte closed her eyes, trying to start at the beginning.

She recalled her childhood clearly. It had been no better or worse than most people's. She remembered Buck Mitchell pinching her backside when they were eight because his older brother dared him to. She'd tied his pants to a flagpole and gave him a wedgie, trying to lift him off the ground in retaliation. Buck learned to respect women a little more after that.

Charlotte remembered when her best friend Lydia asked her to come to work for her in her home-based business, Love Potions, after Lydia's grandmother had died. Annabelle Barratt raised Lydia after her parents died. She might not have been Charlotte's grandmother, but she had been a great influence in her life. Gramma Annabelle had believed in the old magick, not silly magic tricks, but actual magick. She'd taught Lydia and Charlotte that there were things in the universe that could not be explained. She believed there were those who could harness a deep power and control the earth and sky.

Annabelle had sometimes gone off the deep end and had tried to teach them vampire lore, protection spells to ward off evil, and how to avoid stepping into fairy rings, as if those topics had a practical application in everyday life.

Annabelle might have been crazy in some regards, but she'd gotten one thing right. Ghosts were real. Charlotte had seen them, and could rationalize that people transferred their energy into the ether when they died. It also explained why so many people believed in haunting in the modern day. However, Charlotte did not believe in vampires and fairies. If creatures went around entrancing humans and drinking their blood, someone would have surely noticed.

Annabelle was a green witch, a naturalist, which was just another way of saying she was a hippie without the patchouli. She had taught them about herbs and natural remedies. Now Charlotte helped Lydia make teas, candles, lotions, and bath products. Hanging out with her friend all day for work, what could be better than that? It was a dream job.

All that she remembered. Those memories were clear.

Then the new, rich neighbors bought the house on the hill—an old mansion that no one in Green Vallis could afford to upkeep. Like everyone else, Charlotte had been charmed by the

MacGregors with their Scottish accents, charismatic ways, and love of kilts...at first. Now she didn't completely trust them. The feeling of dread she couldn't shake, and her sensation of missing time, both came soon after their arrival. The family was swallowing her hometown whole, buying up property and weaving themselves into the fabric of the small town as if they had always been there.

A MacGregor had even purchased her apartment building. She balled her hand into a fist, thinking of Niall. Like his brothers and cousins—heck, even like the older MacGregor generation—he was more handsome than any man had a right to be, but he was also grumpy and arrogant, and...

Why couldn't she remember? It was right there, on the tip of her lips.

Charlotte felt a tap on her leg and jerked up on the bed. A dark spot wet the knee of her pajama pants. She frowned, instantly looking at the ceiling. Water came through her light fixture and had been dripping on her while she slept. It soaked her leg and her bedspread. She rolled off the mattress with a grimace and glared upward. This apartment used to be her sanctuary. Now it seemed to be falling apart around her.

"Freaking MacGregors," she grumbled.

Pushing the wet pajama pants down her legs, she kicked them aside and grabbed a pair of skinny jeans from the floor and pulled them on. She hopped and wiggled, tugging them up her hips so she could button them.

Charlotte frowned as the water continued to drip on her bed. It quickly became a steady stream. She grabbed the pajama pants and tried to soak up the mess.

Suddenly, a rush of soapy dishwater dumped down onto her. She gasped and scrambled off the bed. The brief waterfall slowed back to a trickle, but the damage had been done. Her mattress was ruined, the ceiling was bowed and cracked, and the light fixture was wet.

Tears of frustration filled her eyes. It was difficult enough trying to sleep without the added bonus of disgusting ceiling water falling on her from the apartment above. All she wanted was to have a normal life back where her biggest concern was too many internet lotion orders.

Warlocks MacGregor® Series

Love Potions
Spellbound
Stirring Up Trouble
Cauldrons and Confessions
Spirits and Spells
Kisses and Curses
Magick and Mischief
A Dash of Destiny
Night Magick

More Coming Soon

About Michelle M. Pillow

New York Times **& *USA TODAY***
Bestselling Author

Michelle loves to travel and try new things, whether it's a paranormal investigation of an old Vaudeville Theatre or climbing Mayan temples in Belize. She believes life is an adventure fueled by copious amounts of coffee.

Newly relocated to the American South, Michelle is involved in various film and documentary projects with her talented director husband. She is mom to a fantastic artist. And she's managed by a dog and cat who make sure she's meeting her deadlines.

For the most part she can be found wearing pajama pants and working in her office. There may or may not be dancing. It's all part of the creative process.

~

Come say hello! Michelle loves talking with readers on social media!

www.MichellePillow.com

facebook.com/AuthorMichellePillow

twitter.com/michellepillow

instagram.com/michellempillow

bookbub.com/authors/michelle-m-pillow

goodreads.com/Michelle_Pillow

amazon.com/author/michellepillow

youtube.com/michellepillow

pinterest.com/michellepillow

Please Leave a Review

THANK YOU FOR READING!

Please take a moment to share your thoughts by reviewing this book.

Be sure to check out Michelle's other titles at www.MichellePillow.com

CPSIA information can be obtained
at www.ICGtesting.com
Printed in the USA
LVHW031031281220
675212LV00023B/247

9 781625 011671